DEVIL ZONE

A JACK NIGHTINGALE SCREENPLAY

By Stephen Leather

Supernatural detective Jack Nightingale appears in the books Nightfall, Midnight, Nightmare, Nightshade, Lastnight, San Francisco Night and New York Night. Before I wrote the novels, I wrote a Jack Nightingale screenplay, Devilzone. To date the film hasn't been made, but I enjoyed the story so much I used it as the basis for the first Jack Nightingale novel, Nightfall.

Stephen Leather

DEVILZONE:

A Jack Nightingale Screenplay

EXT. HOSPITAL - NIGHT

The camera moves towards a hospital. The sign at the entrance has been vandalised.

The camera moves towards the entrance.

INT. HOSPITAL GROUND FLOOR - NIGHT

The camera moves through the hospital. Parts have been vandalised. It's deserted. And in darkness.

INT. HOSPITAL STAIRWELL - NIGHT

The camera moves up the dark stairwell. Plaster is peeling off the damp walls. In the distance, a WOMAN screams.

INT. HOSPITAL UPPER FLOOR - NIGHT

The upper floor is also deserted. Water is dripping from the ceiling.

The WOMAN screams. Then starts to moan.

The camera passes empty rooms. Some of the doors are hanging off their hinges.

Another scream. Blood curdling.

In the distance, lights.

INT. OPERATING THEATRE - NIGHT

The screams and moans are coming from an operating theatre. The doors have been vandalised and there are pools of stagnant water on the floor and a pile of rubble.

But there's an operating table and on it is a YOUNG WOMAN in a hospital gown. She's in pain. And she's giving birth.

The DOCTOR is a man, with bloodshot eyes and unkempt hair, his face hidden behind a surgical mask.

DOCTOR

Come on you bitch.

The WOMAN screams again. There are two NURSES, both in their sixties with hard faces.

DOCTOR

Come on, we haven't got all day.

In the shadows is a MAN dressed in black, his face hidden, smoking a cigar and watching. Around his neck is a chain hanging from which is an inverted pentagram. A Satanic symbol.

The baby arrives. There's a lot of blood. An awful lot of blood.

DOCTOR

About bloody time.

The DOCTOR pulls out the BABY and smacks it, hard.

The BABY cries.

One of the NURSES wraps the BABY in a cloth and gives it to the MAN IN BLACK.

WOMAN

My baby!

The MAN IN BLACK walks away, carrying the child.

WOMAN

MY BABY!!

The DOCTOR throws his bloody surgical gloves onto the floor.

INT. HOSPITAL UPPER FLOOR - NIGHT

The MAN IN BLACK walks along the corridor carrying the BABY. His footsteps echo like gunshots.

INT. HOSPITAL STAIRWELL - NIGHT

The MAN IN BLACK hurries down the stairs, carrying the BABY.

INT. HOSPITAL GROUND FLOOR - NIGHT

The MAN IN BLACK walks quickly along the corridor, holding the BABY. He heads for a rear entrance.

EXT. HOSPITAL REAR ENTRANCE - NIGHT

A MIDDLE-AGED COUPLE are standing outside, waiting fearfully.

A door bangs open.

The MAN IN BLACK is standing there, holding the BABY.

He gives the BABY to the MIDDLE-AGED COUPLE and they hurry over to their car. A 1980s model.

The MAN IN BLACK watches as they drive away with the BABY.

FADE TO BLACK:

                    SOPHIE (V.O.)
Mummy always says that good things happen to good people
and bad things happen to bad people.

FADE IN:

EXT. LONDON HIGH-RISE - DAY

The camera is close up on a pretty nine-year-old girl, SOPHIE.
She has long, curly, blonde hair. SOPHIE is talking to her Barbie
doll.

                    SOPHIE
I don't know what I've done that's so bad, but it must be my
fault.

SOPHIE holds Barbie to her ear and listens intently. Then she
shakes her head.

                    SOPHIE
I can't tell her. She won't believe me. And you know what he
said would happen.

The camera pulls back a little. SOPHIE is sitting on a ledge, the
sky behind her. SOPHIE holds Barbie to her ear again and listens
intently. Then talks to the doll again.

                    SOPHIE
They wouldn't believe me, you know they wouldn't. And
they'd say the same. They'd say that I'm a bad girl and that
it's my fault.

SOPHIE holds Barbie to her ear again, listens, and then nods.

                    SOPHIE
I know you do. I love you, too. I always will. I'm glad you're
here. I'm never scared when you're with me.

The camera pulls back and points down. SOPHIE is sitting on the top of an upmarket tower block. The Thames is in the distance. And the London Eye.

Down below are two police cars and an ambulance. There's a crowd of onlookers being moved back by UNIFORMED PCs.

Among the onlookers is a YOUNG GIRL standing next to a COLLIE DOG. The girl is pale skinned with long dark hair, pretty with lots of black eye-shadow and lipstick, dressed all in black. Lots of piercings. She's PROSERPINE, but at this stage she's just a face in the crowd.

Everyone is staring up at SOPHIE.

EXT. STREET, POLICE P.O.V. - DAY

Two UNIFORMED POLICEMEN are standing either side of a FOREIGN AU PAIR, staring up at SOPHIE. Both POLICEMEN are in their early twenties.

                    FOREIGN AU PAIR
Why don't you do something?

                    FIRST POLICEMAN
We have to wait for the negotiator.

                    FOREIGN AU PAIR
                    (crossing herself)
Oh God, oh God, Oh God.

                    SECOND POLICEMAN
                    (into radio)
Six four eight to control, where is the negotiator, Sarge?

                    SERGEANT (V.O.)
On his way. What's happening there?

SECOND POLICEMAN
It doesn't look good, Sarge.

FOREIGN AU PAIR
Oh God, Oh God, Oh God. Let me go up and talk to her.
(shouting)
Sophie! Sophie it's me! Go back inside! Don't do anything...
(stupid...)

The FIRST POLICEMAN grabs her arm.

FIRST POLICEMAN
Please, miss. You don't know what might set her off. Wait
until the professionals get here.

FOREIGN AU PAIR
I'm supposed to be looking after her.

FIRST POLICEMAN
Please, miss. Getting upset won't help anyone.

FOREIGN AU PAIR
You'll tell Mr and Mrs Underwood that it wasn't my fault,
won't you?

A car pulls up. There's a man driving. Good-looking. Confident.
Thirty years old. He's JACK NIGHTINGALE. Inspector Jack
Nightingale, the Met's most successful hostage negotiator. Nice
suit. Gleaming shoes.

SECOND POLICEMAN
(into radio)
Inspector Nightingale's just arrived, Sarge.

NIGHTINGALE gets out of his car and looks up at SOPHIE.

The FIRST POLICEMAN goes over to NIGHTINGALE.
NIGHTINGALE gives him a curt nod.

NIGHTINGALE
Talk to me.

NIGHTINGALE starts to walk quickly towards the tower block.
The POLICEMAN hurries to keep up with him.

FIRST POLICEMAN
Her name's Sophie Underwood. Nine years old. Family lives
in the penthouse. Top floor.

NIGHTINGALE
I know what a penthouse is.

A UNIFORMED WPC has the door open for them.
NIGHTINGALE walks into the tower block, followed by the
FIRST POLICEMAN.

INT. TOWER BLOCK LOBBY - DAY

The FIRST POLICEMAN heads for the lifts.

NIGHTINGALE nods at the stairs.

NIGHTINGALE
Stairs.

The FIRST POLICEMAN looks confused.

NIGHTINGALE
I hate lifts.

INT. TOWER BLOCK STAIRWELL - DAY

NIGHTINGALE hurries up the stairs. The FIRST POLICEMAN
follows close behind. NIGHTINGALE is as fit as a butcher's dog,
the FIRST POLICEMAN is soon out of breath. They talk as they
climb.

FIRST POLICEMAN

Au pair noticed Sophie wasn't in the flat and thought she might have gone downstairs. There's a communal garden at the back. Swings and stuff. Then she looked up and saw her on the ledge. She started screaming and we heard her.

NIGHTINGALE

The girl or the au pair screamed?

FIRST POLICEMAN

The au pair. The girl seems calm. Talking to her doll most of the time.

NIGHTINGALE

Did the au pair say the girl was worried? Angry? Had they argued?

FIRST POLICEMAN

No, sir. She left her watching television while she did the ironing.

NIGHTINGALE

Why wasn't she at school?

FIRST POLICEMAN

I don't know, sir.

NIGHTINGALE

You didn't ask the au-pair?

FIRST POLICEMAN
(embarrassed)

I didn't think...I'm sorry.

NIGHTINGALE

Parents?

FIRST POLICEMAN
Father works in the city. Banking. Au pair isn't sure of the
name of his firm. She's only been in the UK for a month.
Mother's out shopping. We've called her mobile but it was
busy. We've left a message.

EXT. THE ROOF - DAY

They reach the roof. NIGHTINGALE looks uncomfortable.

NIGHTINGALE
I hate heights.
(a beat)
Has the girl done this before?

FIRST POLICEMAN
Au pair says no but she wouldn't know, she's only...

NIGHTINGALE
...been in the country for a month. Yeah, you said. Have you
run them through the PNC, the parents?

FIRST POLICEMAN
Speeding fines, nothing else.

EXT. THE LEDGE - DAY

SOPHIE is listening to Barbie. She frowns, then talks to the doll.

SOPHIE
There's no need to be scared. I'm here.

There's the sound of a door opening. SOPHIE turns around and
sees NIGHTINGALE walk out onto the flat roof.

The FIRST POLICEMAN walks out behind NIGHTINGALE,
but NIGHTINGALE waves him back.

Then NIGHTINGALE slowly walks over to SOPHIE, talking as he walks.

NIGHTINGALE

Hello Sophie. It's a beautiful day, isn't it?

SOPHIE

Who are you?

NIGHTINGALE

My name's Jack.

SOPHIE

Like Jack and the beanstalk?

NIGHTINGALE

Yeah, but I don't have my beanstalk with me today. I had to use the stairs.

SOPHIE

Why didn't you use the lift?

NIGHTINGALE

I don't like lifts.

SOPHIE puts the doll next to her ear and listens.
NIGHTINGALE stops about a dozen steps away from SOPHIE.

SOPHIE stops listening to the doll.

SOPHIE

Jessica doesn't like lifts, either.

NIGHTINGALE

That's a nice name, Jessica.

SOPHIE

Jessica Lovely, that's her full name. What's your full name?

NIGHTINGALE
Nightingale. Jack Nightingale.

SOPHIE
Like the bird?

NIGHTINGALE
That's right. Like the bird.

SOPHIE
I wish I was a bird.

SOPHIE looks across the skyline.

SOPHIE
I wish I could fly.

NIGHTINGALE
It's not so much fun, being a bird.

SOPHIE frowns, wondering what he means.

NIGHTINGALE
They can't swim, they can't play video games, and they have
to eat off the floor.

SOPHIE smiles.

Suddenly there's a siren. SOPHIE jumps.

NIGHTINGALE
It's okay. It's a fire engine.

SOPHIE
I thought it was the police.

NIGHTINGALE
They have different sirens.

The siren fades in the distance.

NIGHTINGALE
A fire engine sounds like this.

NIGHTINGALE makes a noise like a fire engine siren.

NIGHTINGALE
And this is a police car.

NIGHTINGALE makes a noise like a police siren.

SOPHIE laughs.

NIGHTINGALE
Is it okay if I sit down?

SOPHIE
It's up to you. It's a free country.

NIGHTINGALE sits down on the ledge, some distance away from SOPHIE.

Down below, the POLICE and ONLOOKERS are staring up.

SOPHIE
You're a policeman, aren't you?

NIGHTINGALE
How did you know?

SOPHIE looks at him as if he's stupid.

SOPHIE
The policeman down there said hello to you.

NIGHTINGALE smiles at her powers of observation.

NIGHTINGALE
Yes, I'm a policeman.

SOPHIE
Am I in trouble?

NIGHTINGALE
No, you're not in trouble. We just want to make sure you're okay.

SOPHIE scowls. She's clearly not okay.

NIGHTINGALE
The girl who looks after you, what's her name?

SOPHIE
Inga. She's from Latvia.

NIGHTINGALE
She's worried about you.

SOPHIE
She's stupid.

NIGHTINGALE
Why do you say that?

SOPHIE
She can't even use the microwave.

EXT. STREET, POLICE P.O.V. - DAY

The FOREIGN AU PAIR is looking up with the SECOND POLICEMAN.

FOREIGN AU PAIR
He should just grab her.

SECOND POLICEMAN
It's too risky.

FOREIGN AU PAIR
Why doesn't he do something?

SECOND POLICEMAN
He is doing something. He's talking to her.

EXT. THE LEDGE - DAY

NIGHTINGALE takes out a pack of cigarettes and a lighter.

> NIGHTINGALE
> Is it okay if I smoke?

> SOPHIE
> They're your lungs.

NIGHTINGALE looks surprised - that's a very adult thing to say.

> SOPHIE
> That's what mum says to my dad.

NIGHTINGALE lights a cigarette.

> NIGHTINGALE
> I'm trying to give up.

SOPHIE's skirt has ridden up. NIGHTINGALE sees a bruise on her leg.

> NIGHTINGALE
> What happened to your leg?

> SOPHIE
> (quickly)
> Nothing.

SOPHIE pulls her skirt down over the bruise.

NIGHTINGALE blows smoke.

> NIGHTINGALE
> Isn't today a school day?

> SOPHIE
> Mummy said I didn't have to go.

NIGHTINGALE

Are you poorly?

SOPHIE

Not really.
(a beat)
I am in trouble, aren't I?

NIGHTINGALE

No. I promise you, you're not.

SOPHIE

Have you got any children?

NIGHTINGALE
(shaking his head)

I'm not married.

SOPHIE

You don't have to be married to have children.

SOPHIE starts to cry.

NIGHTINGALE

What's wrong, Sophie?

SOPHIE

Nothing.

NIGHTINGALE moves closer to SOPHIE but she holds up a hand, warding him off.

SOPHIE

Don't touch me!

NIGHTINGALE

I wasn't going to touch you, Sophie.

SOPHIE

I don't want to be touched. By anyone.

NIGHTINGALE smokes his cigarette. SOPHIE is still crying.

> NIGHTINGALE
>
> Maybe I can help.

> SOPHIE
>
> No one can help me.

> NIGHTINGALE
>
> I can try.

> SOPHIE
>
> He said they'd take me away. Put me in care.

> NIGHTINGALE
>
> Your father?

SOPHIE wipes tears away.

> SOPHIE
>
> He said they'd blame me. He said they'd take me away and make me live in a home and that everyone would say it was my fault.

> NIGHTINGALE
> (off her bruised leg)
>
> Did he do that?

SOPHIE nods, still brushing away the tears.

> NIGHTINGALE
>
> Come with me, Sophie. We'll talk to your mother.

SOPHIE stops wiping her tears. She looks at him coldly.

> SOPHIE
>
> She already knows.

They share a long look as NIGHTINGALE realises what the little girl is going through.

> SOPHIE

You can't help me.

SOPHIE looks out across the skyline. A distant look in her eyes.

> SOPHIE

No one can help me.

NIGHTINGALE realises that she's going to jump. He reaches for her, but she slips silently off the ledge, clutching her doll.

> NIGHTINGALE

Sophie!

EXT. STREET, POLICE P.O.V. - DAY

SOPHIE falls from the ledge.

The FOREIGN AU PAIR screams.

The SECOND POLICEMAN turns away in horror.

EXT. THE LEDGE - DAY

NIGHTINGALE stands up, horrified by what he's seen.

EXT. TOWER BLOCK - DAY

NIGHTINGALE walks out of the tower block, his face hard.

SOPHIE's body is being wheeled to an ambulance by two PARAMEDICS.

Another car has arrived. It's ROBBIE HOYLE, a thirty-something police officer who is also a negotiator and a close friend of NIGHTINGALE's.

                        HOYLE
        Jack, the Super wants you to call him.

NIGHTINGALE walks past HOYLE, saying nothing.

                        HOYLE
          Urgent, he said.

HOYLE watches as NIGHTINGALE gets into his car and drives
off at speed.

PROSERPINE and her COLLIE DOG are also watching.

EXT. LONDON BANK - DAY

NIGHTINGALE pushes through the door into the lobby of a
large City bank.

INT. CORRIDOR, LONDON BANK - DAY

NIGHTINGALE walks down a corridor, his face hard.

He reaches a door marked 'Richard Underwood, Head of Retail
Development'.

NIGHTINGALE bangs through the door.

INT. UNDERWOOD'S OUTER OFFICE - DAY

A SECRETARY guards the inner sanctum. She looks up as
NIGHTINGALE crashes through the door.

She frowns, confused.

                     SECRETARY
          And you are...?

Hardly breaking stride, NIGHTINGALE flashes his warrant card.

NIGHTINGALE

Police.

SECRETARY

You can't go in without...

Too late. He throws open the door to UNDERWOOD's office. He storms in and slams the door shut behind him.

The SECRETARY reaches for her phone.

SECRETARY

Security?

EXT. LONDON BANK - DAY

The camera pans up the outside of the bank building. It's a bright, sunny day.

CRASH! One of the windows explodes in a shower of glass as RICHARD UNDERWOOD bursts through and falls to his death.

EXT. QUIET STREET- NIGHT

It's raining. The camera finds a parked car. A battered old MGB. A classic.

INT. NIGHTINGALE'S CAR - NIGHT

NIGHTINGALE is sitting in the driving seat. He is using a video camera, videoing something going on outside.

CAPTION: 'TWO YEARS LATER'

EXT. QUIET STREET - NIGHT

NIGHTINGALE gets out of the car. He walks along the street, towards a detached house. He's more disheveled than the first time we saw him. He's wearing a cheap raincoat and well-worn Hush Puppies.

He shelters under a tree and videos the house. A bedroom light goes on.

A WOMAN appears at the window. Then a MAN. They kiss. He undresses her. NIGHTINGALE keeps videoing.

INT. NIGHTINGALE'S OFFICE - DAY

The office is in a cheap rent area of London. It's a shabby private detective agency. One desk is Nightingale's. Piled high with papers, dirty coffee cups, an ash tray overflowing with cigarette butts.

Nightingale's secretary, twenty-something JENNY SCOTT, is alone in the office, working on her word processor. Her desk is clean and tidy. She's pretty and has a cut-glass accent.

The door opens and NIGHTINGALE walks in carrying his video recorder. He plonks it on to JENNY's desk.

                    NIGHTINGALE
    Caught the little bugger with his pants down. Served him
    right. If you're going to fool around, you should at least draw
    the curtains.

NIGHTINGALE sits down at his desk, pulls open the bottom drawer of the desk and takes out a bottle of whisky. He pours a good slug into the least filthy of the coffee cups.

JENNY looks at him disdainfully as he drinks.

                    NIGHTINGALE
    What? Hair of the dog.

JENNY picks up her notebook.

> JENNY
> Solicitor down in Surrey wants a meeting. Said it was
> something to your advantage.

> NIGHTINGALE
> A job?

> JENNY
> I assume so. I asked if he could come here but he said he has
> trouble with his leg. Gout. I said you'd go and see him. It's
> not as if you've much on at the moment.

NIGHTINGALE flashes JENNY a tight smile. He knows he
doesn't have much work on.

INT. NIGHTINGALE'S CAR ON A COUNTRY ROAD - DAY

NIGHTINGALE drives down a country road. It's pouring with
rain.

He stops at a crossroads and looks at a signpost. One of the signs
points towards 'HAMDALE, 5 miles'. He heads towards the
village.

EXT. COUNTRY ROAD - DAY

NIGHTINGALE drives down the road in the pouring rain.

There's a scarecrow in a field he drives by, its old clothes
flapping in the wind.

Standing next to the scarecrow is a soaking wet GIRL with long
blonde hair that is plastered to her skin. The GIRL'S face is
hidden by her hair. It might be SOPHIE. Or SOPHIE's ghost. Or
just something that looks like SOPHIE. She's wearing a long
white dress. Her hands are hanging lifelessly at her sides.

NIGHTINGALE doesn't notice the scarecrow. Or the GIRL.

EXT. BRIDGE OVER RIVER- DAY

NIGHTINGALE drives over a bridge. The rain is still pouring down and he can barely see.

EXT. COUNTRY ROAD - DAY

NIGHTINGALE drives down a narrow road.

INT. NIGHTINGALE'S CAR - DAY

Ahead, at the side of the road NIGHTINGALE sees a figure. It's a TRAMP, soaking wet from the rain.

NIGHTINGALE frowns. The TRAMP is mouthing something. He's actually saying 'You're going straight to hell, Nightingale,' but all he can see is his lips moving.

NIGHTINGALE twists around in his seat as the car goes past the TRAMP.

He's not there. NIGHTINGALE frowns. Did he imagine it?

NIGHTINGALE turns to look back at the road.

A tractor pulls out of a side road, almost hitting NIGHTINGALE's car.

                    NIGHTINGALE
     Jesus Christ!

NIGHTINGALE slams on the brakes. The car screeches to a halt.

NIGHTINGALE twists around. There's no sign of the tractor. He frowns. Was it ever there?

NIGHTINGALE starts driving again.

EXT. COUNTRY ROAD - DAY

NIGHTINGALE drives through the pouring rain.

He passes a signpost. 'HAMDALE'.

EXT. HAMDALE VILLAGE - DAY

NIGHTINGALE parks his car.

He gets out and hurries through the rain towards a small
solicitor's office.

He opens the door to the office and hurries inside.

INT. SOLICITOR'S OFFICE - DAY

An ELDERLY SECRETARY looks up as NIGHTINGALE
hurries in, dripping wet. The office is old fashioned, files piled
everywhere.

> SOLICITOR'S SECRETARY
> Oh, is it still raining?

NIGHTINGALE flashes her a tight smile.

> NIGHTINGALE
> Jack Nightingale, I'm here to see Mr Turtledove.

The door to the inner office opens and a portly, sixty-something
man offers his hand to NIGHTINGALE. He has a walking stick.

> TURTLEDOVE
> Ernest Turtledove, Mr Nightingale. It's still raining, is it?

Another tight smile from NIGHTINGALE.

> TURTLEDOVE

Please, come on through.

INT. TURTLEDOVE'S OFFICE - DAY

TURTLEDOVE ushers NIGHTINGALE into his office. It's even untidier than the outside office. A real mess. NIGHTINGALE has to step over files.

> TURTLEDOVE

Coincidence, isn't it?

> NIGHTINGALE

What is?

> TURTLEDOVE

You being a Nightingale. Me a turtledove. Small world.

> NIGHTINGALE

Miniscule.

> TURTLEDOVE

Please, sit down.

TURTLEDOVE drops down onto a chair behind his untidy desk. NIGHTINGALE has to move a stack of files off a chair.

> TURTLEDOVE

First of all, let me say how sorry I am for your loss.

> NIGHTINGALE
> (confused)

My loss?

> TURTLEDOVE

Your father.

> NIGHTINGALE
> (even more confused)

My father?

TURTLEDOVE
That's why you're here, isn't it? Your father's will?

NIGHTINGALE
I thought I was here about work.

TURTLEDOVE looks flustered and confused. NIGHTINGALE
hands over a business card.

NIGHTINGALE
I do a lot of work for solicitors. I thought that was why you
wanted to see me.

TURTLEDOVE shakes his head as he sorts through papers and
files on his desk.

TURTLEDOVE
Oh no, no, no. Where is it now? Ah, here we are.

TURTLEDOVE holds up a legal document. A will.

TURTLEDOVE
Your father's will.

NIGHTINGALE
My parents died ten years ago. Their estate was settled at the
time.

Now TURTLEDOVE is confused. He puts on a pair of thick
spectacles, reads a letter and looks at the will, muttering to
himself.

TURTLEDOVE
That can't be right, let me see, let me see. No, here it is. Jack
Nightingale.

TURTLEDOVE hands across a sheet of paper.

TURTLEDOVE

This is you, isn't it? Correct date of birth, national insurance number, school record.

NIGHTINGALE frowns as he reads the sheet of paper.

NIGHTINGALE

That's me all right.

TURTLEDOVE

So there's no mistake then. This is the last will and testament of Ainsley Gosling. Your father.

NIGHTINGALE
(shaking his head)
My father's name was George Nightingale. I've seen my birth certificate. George and Irene Nightingale.

TURTLEDOVE

You were adopted, Mr Nightingale. Shortly after you were born.

NIGHTINGALE

Bollocks.

TURTLEDOVE looks over the top of his glasses.

TURTLEDOVE

There's no need for profanity, Mr Nightingale. I can understand this might well be a shock, but I am only the messenger.

NIGHTINGALE

I'm sorry. But I've never heard of - what did you say his name was?

TURTLEDOVE

Gosling. Ainsley Gosling. And you are his sole heir. There's that bird thing again. Nightingale. Turtledove. Gosling. A veritable aviary.

NIGHTINGALE is shocked. Shocked and confused.

> NIGHTINGALE
>
> How did he die?

> TURTLEDOVE
>
> I don't know. I received a communication saying that Mr Gosling had passed away and that I was to pass the will on to you.

TURTLEDOVE hands over the will. NIGHTINGALE looks at it.

> TURTLEDOVE
>
> There is little in the way of cash, I'm afraid. A few thousand pounds at most, once my fees have been taken into account. But there is a substantial property.

INT. NIGHTINGALE'S CAR - DAY

NIGHTINGALE drives along the driveway to Gosling's house. It's a big house, a modern mansion, with floor to ceiling mirrored windows all around. The rain has stopped but the house is still glistening wet.

> TURTLEDOVE (V.O.)
>
> A house. Quite an impressive dwelling actually. Your father's last remaining asset.

EXT. GOSLING'S HOUSE - DAY

NIGHTINGALE climbs out of his car and stands looking up at the house.

> NIGHTINGALE
>
> Nice.

He sees CCTV cameras covering the entrance to the house.

He sees his reflection in the glass walls. It's very disconcerting.

He walks up to the house and presses his hand against the glass, trying to see inside. All he can see is his reflection.

Suddenly he gets the feeling that there's somebody behind him, but when he whirls around there's no one there.

NIGHTINGALE has a key, given to him by TURTLEDOVE. He pushes open the door.

INT. HALLWAY, GOSLING'S HOUSE - DAY

The hallway is huge with a massive staircase and a modern chandelier. There's hardly any furniture. Glossy wooden floors everywhere. And floor to ceiling glass walls.

There's a CCTV camera in the hallway.

As NIGHTINGALE shuts the door, he realises that he can see right through the glass walls. They are giant one-way mirrors allowing those inside to see out, but impenetrable from the outside.

He looks out over the dark garden. It's very disconcerting, almost as if there's no wall there.

INT. RECEPTION ROOM, GOSLING'S HOUSE - DAY

NIGHTINGALE walks through a huge reception room. The room is virtually bare, it's been stripped of its furniture and paintings. But there's a huge fireplace, and above it, a mirror.

There's a CCTV camera in one corner.

Propped up against the mirror is an envelope. On the envelope is written 'JACK NIGHTINGALE'.

NIGHTINGALE stands looking at the envelope. The camera pans around so that it's looking through the glass wall.

Standing in the middle of the garden is the GIRL. Her head is down so that her blonde, curly hair is hanging down over her face. Her arms are hanging lifelessly at her sides.

NIGHTINGALE doesn't see her. He picks up the envelope.

Upstairs, he hears a noise. A scraping sound.

INT. HALLWAY, GOSLING'S HOUSE - DAY

NIGHTINGALE moves cautiously up the stairs.

INT. LANDING, GOSLING'S HOUSE - DAY

NIGHTINGALE moves along the landing.

There are spaces on the walls where there used to be paintings. The floors are bare, gleaming wood.

NIGHTINGALE listens at one of the bedroom doors. Nothing. Down the landing, he hears the noise again. He takes a deep breath and heads towards the noise.

NIGHTINGALE reaches the door where he thought the noise was coming from. He listens at the door. Then takes a deep breath and throws the door open.

INT. BEDROOM, GOSLING'S HOUSE - DAY

NIGHTINGALE stands in the doorway. There's no furniture. But there are lots of candles in candlesticks. Big candles, the type used in churches. The floor is gleaming wood, the walls all glass.

The candles surround something that has been drawn on the wooden floor. A white star. NIGHTINGALE looks at it. It's not a star. It's a pentangle. Surrounded by a circle.

Suddenly there's movement - a black cat dashes out of the corner of the room, scaring NIGHTINGALE.

The cat rushes out of the room.

NIGHTINGALE frowns as he sees a stain on the wooden floor. He kneels and stares at a rusty-coloured patch. He rubs it. Smells it. It could be dried blood.

                    FIRST PC (O.S.)
    What the hell are you doing?

The voice startles NIGHTINGALE. Big time.

There are two UNIFORMED POLICE OFFICERS standing in the doorway. One has his baton drawn.

                    NIGHTINGALE
    My name's Nightingale. Jack Nightingale. I'm a PI.

                    FIRST PC
    I didn't ask who you were. Or what you are. I want to know what the hell you think you're doing here.

                    NIGHTINGALE
    It's my house.

                    FIRST PC
    Yeah, and I'm the queen of England.

                    NIGHTINGALE
    I used to be in the job. In another life.

                    SECOND PC
                    (suspiciously)
    Where?

                    NIGHTINGALE
    The Met.

NIGHTINGALE takes out a business card. The SECOND
POLICEMAN takes it.

> NIGHTINGALE

I'm freelance now.

> SECOND PC
> (off the card, with contempt)

A private dick.

> NIGHTINGALE

We can't all be high-flyers.

> FIRST PC

And what are you doing here, Mr Nightingale?

> NIGHTINGALE

It's my house. Apparently. I just inherited it.
> (off the bloodstain)

That's blood, yeah?

> FIRST PC

That's where old man Gosling killed himself. Blew his head
off with a shotgun.

> SECOND PC

It was us got into the house. He'd been dead a week. Old man
Gosling hardly ever left the place.

> NIGHTINGALE

There's no doubt that it was suicide?

> FIRST PC

The shotgun was still in his hands. Are you going to be
moving in?

> NIGHTINGALE
> (laughing)

Into here? You're joking.

> FIRST PC
> (Off the envelope)

What's that?

> NIGHTINGALE

It was left here for me.

NIGHTINGALE opens the envelope. Inside is a key. And a business card for a safe deposit company.

INT. SAFE DEPOSIT BOX COMPANY - DAY

NIGHTINGALE follows a CLERK down a staircase.

The CLERK uses his key to open a safe deposit box. Then he shows NIGHTINGALE how to use his key.

> CLERK

I'll leave you to it, Mr Nightingale. Let me know when you've finished.

The CLERK walks away as NIGHTINGALE opens the box.

Inside the box is a DVD.

INT. NIGHTINGALE'S OFFICE - DAY

JENNY is on the phone.

> JENNY
> (into phone)

I'm sure that the cheque was sent out on Wednesday.

JENNY frowns at NIGHTINGALE as he walks in carrying the DVD. She wags a warning finger at him.

JENNY
(into phone)
He isn't in at the moment, but as soon as he gets in I'll get him to call you. Absolutely. Good bye.

JENNY hangs up.

JENNY
The bank.

NIGHTINGALE hands her the DVD and nods at her computer.

JENNY
Jack, I can't keep lying to them forever.

She slots the DVD into her computer and clicks the mouse.

NIGHTINGALE
It's a cashflow problem.

The DVD plays. There's a man on screen. A man in his early seventies. A man who looks haunted, at the end of his tether. AINSLEY GOSLING. He's the MAN IN BLACK we saw in the hospital. But much older. Life hasn't been good to him. Around his neck is the chain with the inverted pentagram.

GOSLING forces a smile at the camera.

GOSLING
Hello Jack. I wish that this could have been under more fortuitous circumstances, but....

GOSLING shrugs. Lost for words.

GOSLING
The fact that you're watching this means that I'm already dead.

JENNY
What is this?

NIGHTINGALE shakes his head and frowns at her.

> GOSLING
>
> Nothing I can say will ever make up for what I've
> condemned you to.

> JENNY
>
> Jack?

> NIGHTINGALE
>
> Shhh.

> GOSLING
>
> But you must believe me, I do regret my actions...if I could
> turn back time...but what's done is done.

GOSLING takes a deep breath, and prepares to bare his soul.

> GOSLING
>
> I'm your father, Jack. But I suppose that's already been
> explained to you. Not that being your father means anything,
> not in the traditional sense. I've given you nothing over the
> last thirty-two years. Not even your name.

GOSLING is looking increasingly uncomfortable. He pours
himself a brandy with a shaking hand.

> GOSLING
>
> I gave you away when you were one day old, Jack. Gave you
> to the Nightingales. I knew they were good people.
> (with a rueful smile)
> God-fearing people.

> JENNY
>
> What the hell is this?

> NIGHTINGALE
>
> Shhh.

JENNY gets up and goes over to the coffee-maker. She makes coffee as GOSLING continues to talk.

> GOSLING
>
> So. Where do I start? At the beginning or the end? Do I tell you what happened? Or what's going to happen?

GOSLING drains his glass and pours himself another brandy.

> GOSLING
>
> On your thiry-third birthday, a demon from hell is coming to claim your soul.

JENNY drops her coffee mug and it shatters, startling NIGHTINGALE. JENNY rushes next to NIGHTINGALE and stares at the television set.

> JENNY
>
> Who is that?

> NIGHTINGALE
>
> My father.

> JENNY
>
> Your father's dead.

> NIGHTINGALE
> (watching the TV)
>
> Shhh.

> GOSLING
>
> I did a deal, thirty-three years ago. A deal with a devil. Not the devil. One of his minions.

> JENNY
>
> This is a joke, right?

GOSLING

The deal was simple. I got power. Almost unlimited power.
Power over women. Power to amass money, more money
than I could spend in a hundred lifetimes. The only thing I
couldn't get was immortality. That wasn't up for negotiation.

GOSLING drinks more. His hand still shaking.

JENNY

He's mad. Insane. Look at him.

NIGHTINGALE isn't listening. He lights a cigarette.

GOSLING

In exchange for your immortal soul, I got the keys to the
kingdom here on earth. And now it's time to pay the piper.

GOSLING pours more brandy.

GOSLING

I've tried to put this right. I tried to renegotiate, but there's
nothing I can do. What's done is done. Your soul is forfeit.

GOSLING smiles ruefully.

GOSLING

I just wanted you to know that I'm sorry. Sorry for what I
did, sorry for what happened. And sorry for what's going to
happen to you.

GOSLING reaches for something. A shotgun. He places the end
of the barrel in his mouth and uses his toe to pull the trigger.
BANG! Blows his head to bits. Blood everywhere.

The DVD comes to an end.

JENNY and NIGHTINGALE are stunned.

JENNY

Jack, what's going on?

> NIGHTINGALE

I don't know.

> JENNY

Your birthday's next week.

INT. TURTLEDOVE'S OFFICE - DAY

TURTLEDOVE is reading a file and stirring a cup of tea.

He dips in a biscuit. The door crashes open. It's NIGHTINGALE. Part of TURTLEDOVE's biscuit drops into his tea.

> NIGHTINGALE

What the hell is going on?

> TURTLEDOVE

Excuse me?

> NIGHTINGALE

Who the hell is Ainsley Gosling?

> TURTLEDOVE

I'm not sure I like your tone, Mr Nightingale.

> NIGHTINGALE

This Gosling. Who is he?

> TURTLEDOVE

I never met the man. Everything was dealt with by courier.

> NIGHTINGALE

You witnessed the will. You must have met him.

TURTLEDOVE looks pained.

                         TURTLEDOVE
It's a little irregular, I know, but I didn't actually witness the
signing. I drew up the will, it was couriered to Mr Gosling,
he signed it and it was couriered back. So far as I'm aware,
he never left the house.

  NIGHTINGALE sits down.

                         NIGHTINGALE
Who is he?

                         TURTLEDOVE
He's not my client. The will was the only business I did for
him. I drew up the will, and when I was notified of his
demise, I contacted you.

                         NIGHTINGALE
You didn't leave an envelope there for me?

  TURTLEDOVE shakes his head, mystified.

                         NIGHTINGALE
But you were paid? For the work you did.

                         TURTLEDOVE
Obviously.

                         NIGHTINGALE
By cheque?

EXT. BANK - DAY

Establishing shot of a bank branch.

INT. BANK MANAGER'S OFFICE - DAY

NIGHTINGALE is shaking hands with the BANK MANAGER.

BANK MANAGER
I'm not sure how I can help, Mr Nightingale.

NIGHTINGALE
I'm heir to Ainsley Gosling's estate.

BANK MANAGER
I understand that, but as I said on the phone, your late
father's accounts are all closed.

NIGHTINGALE sits down. So does the BANK MANAGER.

NIGHTINGALE
What happened to his money?

BANK MANAGER
I'm not sure I'm at liberty to divulge the details of your late
father's estate.

NIGHTINGALE
I'm his sole heir. I don't see that it would be a problem to get
access to your records through the courts. But all I want is to
know what happened to his money. The house must be worth
a small fortune.

BANK MANAGER
I gather it's heavily mortgaged. But I would assume that if
you were to sell it, there would be something left after taxes,
yes.

NIGHTINGALE
And all the furniture has gone.

BANK MANAGER
Your late father sold the contents, that's my understanding.

NIGHTINGALE
Which brings me back to my question - what happened to his
money?

                        BANK MANAGER
He made substantial withdrawals in the latter years of his
life. What he spent it on, well, that's his business, isn't it?

                        NIGHTINGALE
How much was there? Before he started spending?

The BANK MANAGER taps away on his desktop computer. He
studies a spreadsheet.

                        BANK MANAGER
Three years ago your father had close to... eight million
pounds in cash.

                        NIGHTINGALE
What...

                        BANK MANAGER
And a further three million in stocks and shares.

NIGHTINGALE looks dumbfounded.

                        NIGHTINGALE
You're telling me that Ainsley Gosling spent eleven million
pounds in three years?

EXT. BANK - DAY

NIGHTINGALE walks out of the bank. He walks along a row of
shops, then he stops and lights a cigarette.

He inhales deeply, then blows smoke.

Across the road is a bus, full of people.

NIGHTINGALE takes another drag on his cigarette, then he
starts walking down the road again, away from the bank.

As he walks away, the bus drives off. Standing on the pavement is the GIRL, he head down, hands limp at her side, her hair down covering her face. NIGHTINGALE doesn't see her. No one does.

INT. PUB - NIGHT

NIGHTINGALE is standing at the bar, drinking whisky. He lights a cigarette. A hand falls on his shoulder, startling him.

It's ROBBIE HOYLE.

> HOYLE
>
> Jumpy...

> NIGHTINGALE
>
> I'm not jumpy, I just don't like being crept up on, that's all.

> HOYLE
>
> I'd tell you to have a drink to calm you down, but by the look of it you've had a few already.

> NIGHTINGALE
>
> What do you want?

> HOYLE
>
> A Porsche, a time share in Malaga, a mistress with huge breasts, all the normal sort of crap.

> NIGHTINGALE
>
> To drink?

> HOYLE
>
> Pint of best.

> NIGHTINGALE
>
> Grab a seat. What I've got to tell you, you'll be better off sitting down.

INT. PUB - LATER

NIGHTINGALE has finished talking to ROBBIE HOYLE.
Telling him everything.

> HOYLE
>
> He's mad, right? It's some sort of sick practical joke. A last
> laugh before he killed himself.

> NIGHTINGALE
>
> Did you get the stuff?

HOYLE takes out an envelope from his pocket and hands it to
NIGHTINGALE. Inside the envelope, photocopies of a police
report including photographs of the death scene. It's messy. Very
messy. Lots of blood and bone and brain.

> HOYLE
>
> Shotgun in his mouth.

> NIGHTINGALE
>
> There's no doubt it was him?

> HOYLE
>
> His fingerprints were all over the house. And the gun. Eleven
> million pounds? And it's all gone?

> NIGHTINGALE
>
> Yeah.

> HOYLE
>
> Pity.

NIGHTINGALE studies the crime scene.

> NIGHTINGALE
>
> What did you make of the pentangle?

> HOYLE
>
> What?

NIGHTINGALE

The star on the floor. With a circle around it.

HOYLE

Interior design. Who the hell knows? I just got the printouts, it wasn't my case. It wasn't anybody's case. It was suicide. Open and shut. You said you saw it on the DVD, right? You saw him kill himself, that's what you said.

NIGHTINGALE

What happened to the body?

HOYLE

Cremated.
(a beat)
You're not taking this seriously, are you? People don't sell their souls to the devil.

NIGHTINGALE

Not his soul. My soul.

HOYLE frowns at NIGHTINGALE.

HOYLE

You know it's bollocks, right? There's no such thing as the devil.

NIGHTINGALE

I know. If there was a devil there'd be a god, and I've seen nothing over the past thirty-odd years that's convinced me that there's a god. No god, no devil. End of story.

HOYLE

There you go, then. It's bollocks.

NIGHTINGALE

He's left me a huge bloody house in the sticks, Robbie. A mansion.

HOYLE

So you're going up in the world. Well done you.

NIGHTINGALE

Why would he do that if I wasn't his son? It's one hell of an expensive joke.

HOYLE

Okay. Show it to me.

NIGHTINGALE

At night?

HOYLE

You are jumpy.

NIGHTINGALE

The power's off. Bill hasn't been paid.

HOYLE

I've got torches in the car. Come on, you could do with some fresh air.

NIGHTINGALE drains his glass.

EXT. GOSLING'S HOUSE - NIGHT

HOYLE's car pulls up in front of the house. It doesn't look quite as normal at night.

NIGHTINGALE and HOYLE get out of the car. HOYLE is impressed.

He waves at his reflection in the mirrored wall.

HOYLE

You weren't kidding.

NIGHTINGALE

It's got to be worth millions, right?

HOYLE opens the boot and tosses a torch to NIGHTINGALE.

> HOYLE
> Show me around, then.

As they walk to the front door, HOYLE looks up at the CCTV cameras.

INT. HALLWAY, GOSLING'S HOUSE - NIGHT

The front door opens. HOYLE plays the beam of his flashlight over a CCTV camera.

> HOYLE
> Security conscious, wasn't he?

> NIGHTINGALE
> They're all over the place.
> But no alarms. Just cameras.

> HOYLE
> So?

> NIGHTINGALE
> So he wasn't worried about burglars.

> HOYLE
> If you've got CCTV you don't need an alarm. Any burglar would know he'd be filmed and give the place a wide berth.

> NIGHTINGALE
> (sarcastic)
> Yeah, if they weren't wearing masks.

> HOYLE
> What are you getting at?

> NIGHTINGALE
> He was scared of something. But it wasn't burglars.

NIGHTINGALE plays the beam of his torch around the hallway.

> NIGHTINGALE
> I wonder where the monitors are?

> HOYLE
> Bedroom, probably.

> NIGHTINGALE
> No wiring there. And if he left the cameras, why move the monitors?

NIGHTINGALE walks around, checking for wiring from the cameras.

INT. DINING ROOM, GOSLING'S HOUSE - NIGHT

NIGHTINGALE and HOYLE walk through a huge wood-paneled dining room. One wall is glass, overlooking the garden.

There are two CCTV cameras covering the room.

> HOYLE
> He had every room wired up.

NIGHTINGALE plays the beam of his torch over the cameras. Then follows a wire. It disappears behind a wooden panel.

NIGHTINGALE starts to examine the paneling.

> HOYLE
> What are you looking for?

> NIGHTINGALE
> I'm not sure.

HOYLE looks out through the glass wall at the gardens.

NIGHTINGALE moves around the room, examining the wooden panels. Then he presses a carving. A section of paneling slides back revealing a doorway. And stairs leading down.

NIGHTINGALE looks at HOYLE.

INT. BASEMENT, GOSLING'S HOUSE - NIGHT

NIGHTINGALE walks down the stairs to the basement. It's huge, one massive room that covers the entire floor area of the house above.

Unlike the rest of the house, the basement is crammed with furniture. Shelves packed with artifacts, bookcases crammed with books. This place is spooky.

The artifacts are all connected with black magic and witchcraft. The books are all leather-bound and very old.

NIGHTINGALE plays the torch beam around the basement. HOYLE joins him.

> HOYLE
>
> Jesus H Christ.

> NIGHTINGALE
>
> I don't think Jesus has much to do with this.

On one wall are a line of CCTV monitors. No power so they are all blank.

NIGHTINGALE pulls out a book and plays his torch over it. 'SACRIFICE and SELF-MUTILATION'. He opens it. Pictures of animals, and people, being killed and mutilated.

> HOYLE
>
> Jack. There's a generator here.

NIGHTINGALE

A what?

HOYLE

A generator.

There's a loud clunking noise, then a generator fires up and suddenly all the lights go on.

HOYLE walks away from a generator, over to NIGHTINGALE.

NIGHTINGALE

Who's a clever boy, then?

Now they can get a true sense of how big the basement is. It's huge.

NIGHTINGALE walks along the shelves, looking at the weird stuff, all of it witchcraft related.

The CCTV monitors flicker into life.

One of the monitors is covering the hallway. The GIRL is standing in the middle of the hallway, her long blonde hair over her face, her hands hanging lifelessly at her side.

Neither NIGHTINGALE or HOYLE look at the monitors.

NIGHTINGALE picks up a skull that is not quite human. Nearby is a huge ornate mirror, the frame made up of snakes and other scary animals.

HOYLE

This is weird stuff, Jack.

HOYLE picks up a black crystal ball and looks at it.

In the crystal he sees himself, wearing a raincoat. Then he sees himself being hit by a van. BANG!

HOYLE flinches and drops the ball. It rolls across the floor.

NIGHTINGALE

What?

HOYLE

I saw myself in there.

NIGHTINGALE picks up the crystal ball. He pulls a face as he looks at it. Nothing. NIGHTINGALE puts the crystal ball back on its stand.

HOYLE

What is this place?

NIGHTINGALE

You know exactly what it is. A shrine to black magic.

HOYLE

There's no such thing as magic. Smoke and mirrors and superstition, that's all there is. This is the twenty-first century.

NIGHTINGALE

You got married in church, didn't you?

HOYLE

So?

NIGHTINGALE

So, that was a religious ceremony. Before God.

HOYLE

That's different.

NIGHTINGALE

No, what you did in church with Anna was a ceremony with all the paraphernalia of religion.

HOYLE has a look of disbelief on his face.

The camera finds the monitor showing the hallway. The GIRL
has gone. But something moves across one of the other monitors.
It's the GIRL, slowly walking, her face down so that it's covered
by her long curly hair, her arms hanging lifelessly down at her
sides. Then she moves out of view.

NIGHTINGALE

And at William's christening, I had to renounce Satan and all
his works, remember.

HOYLE

They're just words.

NIGHTINGALE

I'm not saying there's anything to it. I'm just saying that
Gosling believed in it, that's all. Maybe that's what drove him
to kill himself.

HOYLE

Let's get out of here.

NIGHTINGALE

You wanted to come.

HOYLE

I mean it, Jack. This place gives me the heebie-jeebies.

NIGHTINGALE can see that HOYLE is serious. He looks
around the basement. There is some seriously scary stuff there.
Statues of demons. Knives. Stuff in specimen jars that look like
they might have been ripped from animals. Or people.

NIGHTINGALE

Okay.

HOYLE heads up the stairs.

NIGHTINGALE looks at one of the desks. There's a book open.
It looks like a journal. Or a diary.

NIGHTINGALE picks it up.

The camera goes close up on one of the monitors. The GIRL is moving towards the CCTV camera so that she gets bigger and bigger on the monitor.

Her head is still down so that her hair covers her face, but it's clear that her skin is a deathly white. Then the monitor goes fuzzy.

EXT. HOYLE'S HOUSE - NIGHT

NIGHTINGALE and HOYLE walk towards the front door of a neat suburban semi.

INT. HOYLE'S SITTING ROOM - NIGHT

NIGHTINGALE drops down on a sofa and lights a cigarette. It's a large open plan room with a staircase leading up stairs.

                         HOYLE
      Beer okay?

ANNA, HOYLE's wife, comes in wearing a dressing gown. She's black and pretty, HOYLE is punching above his weight.

                         ANNA
                      (to HOYLE)
      Keep the noise down yeah, William's only just gone to sleep.

                         HOYLE
      Love you, too.

HOYLE goes to get beers from the kitchen.

                         ANNA
      Hi Jack.

                          NIGHTINGALE
Sorry I kept your man out.

                            ANNA
How's business?

                          NIGHTINGALE
Yeah, it's okay.

                            ANNA
And Jenny?

                          NIGHTINGALE
Fine.

                            ANNA
Asked her out yet?

                          NIGHTINGALE
She's an employee.

                            ANNA
She fancies you something rotten. Why else do you think she
works for you?

                          NIGHTINGALE
                           (grinning)
We're a dynamic company with growth prospects.
                           (serious)
She's a bloody good secretary, I wouldn't want to screw that
up by jumping on her.

HOYLE returns with two bottles of beer.

ANNA takes one of them off HOYLE.

                            ANNA
You not having one then?

ANNA takes a swig from the bottle and HOYLE laughs as he gives the other one to NIGHTINGALE.

> HOYLE
> Jack here's a man of property now.

HOYLE goes to get another beer. ANNA drops down on the sofa next to NIGHTINGALE.

> NIGHTINGALE
> I've been left a house.

> ANNA
> Left?

> NIGHTINGALE
> A relative died.

> ANNA
> Close?

> NIGHTINGALE
> My father.

> ANNA
> Jack!

> NIGHTINGALE
> Somebody claiming to be my father.

HOYLE returns with a beer bottle.

> HOYLE
> Some sort of Satanist.

> ANNA
> What?

> NIGHTINGALE
> The guy was disturbed. He blew his head off with a shotgun.

                    ANNA
But he was your father? Your genetic father.

                 NIGHTINGALE
That's what he claims. Difficult to prove.

                    HOYLE
There's DNA.

                 NIGHTINGALE
Body was cremated. Besides, why lie about something like
that?

                    ANNA
We could ask him.

                 NIGHTINGALE
Who?

                    ANNA
Your father. Your real father. What was his name?

                 NIGHTINGALE
Gosling. Ainsley Gosling. What do you mean, ask him?

                    ANNA
A séance. Hands on a glass. Talking to the dead. Robbie and
I used to do it, years ago.

                    HOYLE
It's a joke. A party game.

                    ANNA
We had some weird messages.

                    HOYLE
There's always someone pushing the glass. Pissing about.

ANNA stands up and goes over to a side table where she picks up
a glass.

ANNA

Wanna give it a go?

INT. HOYLE'S SITTING ROOM - LATER

NIGHTINGALE, HOYLE and ANNA are sitting around a coffee table. Letters have been written on pieces of paper, along with the words YES and NO.

The three of them are sitting with their fingers on an upturned glass.

The lights are off and candles are burning.

NIGHTINGALE

This is stupid.

ANNA

Shhh!

ANNA looks around the room.

ANNA

Is there anybody there?

NIGHTINGALE

You're mad.

HOYLE

Careful, mate. The last person who said she's mad is buried in the back garden.

ANNA scowls at him.

ANNA

Is there anybody there?

The glass slides slowly over to 'YES'.

NIGHTINGALE frowns.

NIGHTINGALE

Give me a break.

ANNA

We want to speak to...

She looks across at NIGHTINGALE for the name.

NIGHTINGALE

Ainsley Gosling.

ANNA

Ainsley Gosling. Is Ainsley Gosling there?

The glass slides to the centre of the table, then back to 'YES'.

ANNA

Do you have a message for us?

The glass slides to the centre of the table, then back to 'YES'.

ANNA

What is it you want to say to us?

NIGHTINGALE stares at the glass as it starts to move from letter to letter.

NIGHTINGALE repeats the letters as they are spelled out.

NIGHTINGALE

S-h-a-g j-e-n-n

NIGHTINGALE realises what's going on.

NIGHTINGALE
(to ANNA)

You're such a pain in the arse.

ANNA laughs and clinks her bottle against HOYLE's.

> HOYLE

Your face.

> NIGHTINGALE

You're a couple of kids.

> HOYLE

You were taking it so seriously.

> NIGHTINGALE

Yeah, right.

> ANNA

You were.

ANNA and HOYLE collapse on the sofa, laughing, as NIGHTINGALE leaves.

The camera finds the GIRL sitting on the staircase, her knees up against her chest, her hair hanging down over her face. No one sees her.

INT. NIGHTINGALE'S OFFICE - DAY

NIGHTINGALE is sitting with his feet on his desk, frowning at the book that he took from the basement of Gosling's House.

JENNY arrives for work and is surprised to see him in the office already.

> JENNY

The early worm....

> NIGHTINGALE

A bit of respect would be nice. Me being management and all.

> JENNY

Have you been here all night?

NIGHTINGALE

Maybe.

JENNY
(off the book)

What's that?

NIGHTINGALE

A bit of light reading. Snag is, I can't make head nor tail of it.

JENNY goes to stand behind NIGHTINGALE and looks at the book.

NIGHTINGALE

It's written backwards, but I still can't read it.

JENNY

It's not backwards. It's mirror writing. Like Leonardo da Vinci used to do.

NIGHTINGALE looks at her, surprised.

JENNY gets a mirror out of her bag and holds it against the book. She's right.

NIGHTINGALE

It's not English, is it? What is it, Italian?

JENNY

Latin.

NIGHTINGALE

Latin?

JENNY

Latin is a language, as dead as dead can be, it killed the ancient Romans and now it's killing me.

NIGHTINGALE

My comprehensive was a bit light on dead languages. Can you translate it?

JENNY

Didn't you read my CV?

NIGHTINGALE

I was too busy looking at your legs.

JENNY examines the first page.

JENNY

It's written by someone called Sebastian Mitchell. There's a date here. 1956.

JENNY frowns as she reads the first few paragraphs.

JENNY

Oh, terrific.

NIGHTINGALE

What?

JENNY

It's about summoning demons. And how to trade with them.

NIGHTINGALE frowns. Is she serious?

INT. WINE BAR - EVENING

JENNY and NIGHTINGALE are sitting at the bar. She's drinking wine, he's on whisky. JENNY has the book.

JENNY

As far as I can tell, it's a diary. Written by somebody called Sebastian Mitchell. The first entry is 1956. The most recent was twelve years ago.

JENNY takes a deep breath.

JENNY

I've only read it in parts, it'll take weeks to translate it all.

NIGHTINGALE can see that JENNY is uncomfortable.

NIGHTINGALE

But...?

JENNY

Mitchell was some sort of Satanist. A devil worshipper.

NIGHTINGALE

Terrific.

JENNY

The book is about summoning demons. A sort of 'how to' book. The pitfalls and perils.

NIGHTINGALE

This just keeps getting better and better, doesn't it?

JENNY

Just because it's written down, doesn't mean it's true. I kept a diary until I was fifteen. Full of adolescent ramblings.

NIGHTINGALE

My father was using the book. It was open in his study.
(a beat)
Is there stuff there about selling souls?

JENNY has a pained look on her face. She nods.

NIGHTINGALE
Souls of children?

JENNY

Jack...it's a handwritten diary. Mitchell could have been as crazy as...

NIGHTINGALE
As my father?

There's an uncomfortable silence.

NIGHTINGALE
What does it say...about selling souls?

JENNY
You have to summon a devil. Not the devil, but one of his minions.

NIGHTINGALE
How do you know which devil to summon?

JENNY
You don't believe any of this, do you?

NIGHTINGALE
Just tell me what the book says.

JENNY
There are 66 princes under the devil, each commanding 6,666 legions. Each legion is made up of 6,666 devils.

NIGHTINGALE tries to do the calculation in his head, frowning.

JENNY
Just under three billion.

NIGHTINGALE
There are three billion devils in hell?

JENNY
Big place. Apparently.
(a beat)
You're not starting to take this seriously, are you?

                         NIGHTINGALE
I don't know. The house is real. Ainsley Gosling committed
suicide. That much is true.

                            JENNY
The fact that he blew his head off shows that he wasn't
thinking rationally. You know how delusional people can
get. You dealt with enough when you were with the Met,
didn't you?

NIGHTINGALE drains his glass and slides off his bar stool.

                            JENNY
   Are you okay?

                         NIGHTINGALE
   I need a cigarette.

                            JENNY
   Do you want company?

                         NIGHTINGALE
   I'm okay.

NIGHTINGALE leaves. JENNY picks up the diary and looks at
it.

EXT. LONDON STREET - NIGHT

NIGHTINGALE walks along a deserted street. He lights a cigarette.

EXT. ANOTHER LONDON STREET - NIGHT

NIGHTINGALE walks past a row of shops, closed for the night.

A YOUNG MAN, probably a drug addict, is wrapped in a
sleeping bag. HOMELESS and HUNGRY' is written on a piece
of cardboard in front of him.

> DRUG ADDICT
Got a cigarette, mister?

NIGHTINGALE gives him a cigarette.

> NIGHTINGALE
You know they give you cancer?

> DRUG ADDICT
Got a light?

NIGHTINGALE lights the cigarette for him. He shivers and smiles his thanks.

> DRUG ADDICT
You're going straight to hell, Nightingale.

NIGHTINGALE flinches. Shocked.

> NIGHTINGALE
What?

> DRUG ADDICT
Have you got any spare change?

NIGHTINGALE frowns. Confused. Then he shakes his head and gives the DRUG ADDICT a handful of change.

> DRUG ADDICT
Thanks, mister. Be lucky.

NIGHTINGALE walks away.

He walks by the GIRL, who is standing in a shop doorway, her hands hanging down at her sides, her face down, covered by her hair. NIGHTINGALE walks right by her but doesn't see her.

INT. MULTI-STORY CAR PARK - NIGHT

NIGHTINGALE walks through a deserted car park.

His footsteps echo. Then as he walks he hears a second set of footsteps. He stops. Just silence. NIGHTINGALE looks around. He's on his own.

He starts walking again. His footsteps echo. After a few seconds, there are more footsteps.

NIGHTINGALE climbs into his car.

INT. NIGHTINGALE'S CAR - NIGHT

NIGHTINGALE puts the keys in the ignition and starts the car.

BANG! Hands slam against the driver's window. A face leers at NIGHTINGALE. It's a FOOTBALL THUG.

BANG! Two more hands slam against the passenger side window. ANOTHER FOOTBALL THUG.

                    FOOTBALL THUG
          You're going straight....(to hell, Nightingale)

Before the THUG can finish, NIGHTINGALE drives away from the FOOTBALL THUGS.

INT. NIGHTINGALE'S CAR DRIVING DOWN THE ROAD - NIGHT

NIGHTINGALE drives down the road. He looks nervously in the rear view mirror. He lights a cigarette as he drives.

INT. NIGHTINGALE'S CAR DRIVING TO GRAVEYARD - NIGHT

NIGHTINGALE drives by a graveyard. He stops the car.

There's a moon, enough light to see by.

The graveyard is next to an old church.

EXT. GRAVEYARD - NIGHT

NIGHTINGALE gets out of his car, stamps on his cigarette butt and walks into the graveyard.

There are lots of old gravestones. Crosses. Stone angels. It's a dark, spooky place, but NIGHTINGALE isn't scared as he walks through the graveyard.

As he walks through the graveyard, the camera finds the GIRL, standing by the church. Her hands are hanging by her sides, her head is down so that her hair covers her face. NIGHTINGALE doesn't see her. Is it SOPHIE? It might be.

NIGHTINGALE finds what he's looking for. A twin grave with a single stone. The gravestone bears the name of his adopted parents - George and Irene Nightingale.

NIGHTINGALE stands looking down at the grave.

                    NIGHTINGALE
     Funny old world, innit?

There's a long pause. An owl hoots.

                    NIGHTINGALE
     Why did you never tell me you weren't my real parents? I
     wouldn't have loved you any less. You'll always be mum and
     dad to me.

NIGHTINGALE takes out a cigarette and lights it. He smiles down at the grave.

                    NIGHTINGALE
     I know, I know. You hate me smoking.

NIGHTINGALE blows smoke, taking care not to blow it at the grave. His face becomes serious.

                    NIGHTINGALE
    Did you know about Gosling? Did you know he was my real
    father? Is that why you never said anything?

There's no reply. Just the impassive faces of the stone angels, watching and listening.

Then there's a voice from behind NIGHTINGALE.

                    PRIEST (O.S.)
    Can I help you?

NIGHTINGALE jumps, then turns to see the PRIEST, an elderly man in clerical garb.

                    NIGHTINGALE
    Jesus H Christ!

                      PRIEST
    Hardly

                    NIGHTINGALE
    Sorry.
                    (off the grave)
    My parents.

                      PRIEST
    You're not a member of my parish, are you?

                    NIGHTINGALE
                    (ruefully)
    A lost sheep.

                      PRIEST
    No one is ever lost. The shepherd will always welcome you
    back.

NIGHTINGALE

You don't mind me…

NIGHTINGALE waves a hand. 'You don't mind me coming here,' is what he means.

PRIEST

We never close.

INT. CHURCH - NIGHT

NIGHTINGALE and the PRIEST walk through the church. Towards the altar. It's very Catholic. Lots of images of Jesus in pain.

NIGHTINGALE

Do you believe in the devil, father?

PRIEST

If one believes in the Lord, you have to believe in the devil.

NIGHTINGALE

Horns and a forked tail?

PRIEST

Not necessarily. But who can doubt that there is evil in the world?

NIGHTINGALE

But is it evil within men? Or is evil an outside force that corrupts?

PRIEST

When there was just Adam and Eve there was no evil. Evil came from without.

NIGHTINGALE

And you believe in all that? The Garden of Eden? The apple? The snake?

                              PRIEST
It's not my faith that needs examining. What is it that's
troubling you?

                          NIGHTINGALE
                            (ruefully)
You don't want to go there.

                              PRIEST
Try me.

NIGHTINGALE pulls a pained face. He takes out his pack of
cigarettes.

                              PRIEST
I'm sorry, we don't allow smoking in here.

                          NIGHTINGALE
One of the deadly sins, yeah?

                              PRIEST
Actually, it's Health and Safety. The church is classed as a
place of work so it's illegal to smoke in the building.

NIGHTINGALE puts the cigarettes away.

                              PRIEST
What the Hell. I'm gasping for a smoke anyway.

NIGHTINGALE takes out the pack, lights a cigarette for the
PRIEST and one for himself. They blow smoke contentedly.

                          NIGHTINGALE
I'm not sure I know what's going on. What's real and what's
irrational fear.
                            (a beat)
Is it possible to sell your soul?

                              PRIEST
To the devil?

NIGHTINGALE nods.

The PRIEST takes a long pull on his cigarette. It's a tough question.

> PRIEST
> We talk of giving one's life to Christ, so there must also be misguided individuals who give themselves over to evil.

> NIGHTINGALE
> And would such a deal be irrevocable?

> PRIEST
> A person can always change his mind. The history of the church is littered with conversions.

> NIGHTINGALE
> But what if there was a contract? A contract with the devil?

The PRIEST starts to look a little worried.

> PRIEST
> It's more a case of coming to believe that Jesus Christ is our Lord the Savior.

> NIGHTINGALE
> But what if your soul is already promised to the devil?

> PRIEST
> I think you're being too literal. One no more signs a contract with the devil than one does with Jesus. It's not a matter of signing on the dotted line. It's a matter of belief.

NIGHTINGALE realises that there is no way the PRIEST is going to understand his dilemma.

> NIGHTINGALE
> I suppose so.

The PRIEST looks up at a figure of Christ on a cross.

PRIEST
The church is always here for you, my son.

When the PRIEST looks back, NIGHTINGALE is walking out of the church.

INT. NIGHTINGALE'S CAR DRIVING DOWN ROAD - NIGHT

NIGHTINGALE is driving down the road, deep in thought.

There's a blue flash and the blip of a siren. Police.

EXT. ROADSIDE - NIGHT

A UNIFORMED TRAFFIC COP hands a breathalyzer to NIGHTINGALE.

NIGHTINGALE looks resigned as he blows into it.

The UNIFORMED TRAFFIC COP looks at the reading. Over the limit.

INT. POLICE CAR - NIGHT

NIGHTINGALE gets into the back of the car.

There's a SECOND TRAFFIC COP in the passenger seat. The SECOND TRAFFIC COP twists around in his seat and grins at NIGHTINGALE. His voice is a deep growl.

SECOND TRAFFIC COP
You're going straight to hell, Nightingale.

NIGHTINGALE
What?

SECOND TRAFFIC COP
(in his normal voice)
We'll secure your car and drive you to the station, Sir. That's
where we'll take a urine sample. Or blood, if you'd prefer.

NIGHTINGALE sits back in the seat. The UNIFORMED
TRAFFIC COP walks back to the police car.

INT. POLICE STATION - NIGHT

A UNIFORMED SERGEANT escorts NIGHTINGALE to a cell.

INT. POLICE CELL - NIGHT

NIGHTINGALE sits on his bunk.

The cell door closes on him.

NIGHTINGALE lies down and stares up at the ceiling.

INT. POLICE STATION CORRIDOR - NIGHT

The camera moves slowly along the deserted corridor, towards
NIGHTINGALE's cell.

INT. POLICE CELL - NIGHT

NIGHTINGALE is asleep. The observation hatch flicks open.

The GIRL is there, her head down, her hair covering her face.

She slowly raises her head. Her eyes are dark patches, her skin
stark white in contrast.

INT. POLICE CELL – SAME TIME

NIGHTINGALE wakes up with a start. The observation hatch is closed. NIGHTINGALE stares at the hatch. He sighs as he realises that he was dreaming.

Then - BANG! - the hatch flicks open. It's the UNIFORMED SERGEANT, checking that he is okay.

The hatch flicks shut.

INT. NIGHTINGALE'S OFFICE - DAY

JENNY is studying the Mitchell book, reading it in a small mirror and translating with the help of a dictionary.

NIGHTINGALE walks in, looking like shit.

> JENNY
> You look terrible.

> NIGHTINGALE
> Thanks.

> JENNY
> Have you slept in those clothes?

NIGHTINGALE flops down into his chair.

> NIGHTINGALE
> Coffee would be nice.

JENNY gets up and goes over to the coffee maker.

> NIGHTINGALE
> I was done for drunk driving.

> JENNY
> Oh Jack...

> NIGHTINGALE
> My own fault.

JENNY

What's going to happen?

NIGHTINGALE

I didn't hit anyone so it'll probably just be a ban. I'm gonna need a bus timetable. How goes the translation?

JENNY

There's some weird stuff in there.

NIGHTINGALE

How weird?

JENNY puts a mug of coffee on NIGHTINGALE's desk.

JENNY

You haven't got a tattoo, have you?

NIGHTINGALE

What?

JENNY

A tattoo. Or a mark. In the book he says that anyone whose soul belongs to the devil has a mark. A pentangle. Hidden somewhere on the body.

NIGHTINGALE pulls a face.

JENNY

If you haven't got a mark, then there's nothing to worry about.

NIGHTINGALE

And if I have?

JENNY

You said you hadn't.

NIGHTINGALE
But if I had. Do you think I'd have something to worry about
then?

JENNY
I think it's the ramblings of a disturbed mind. A sad bastard
with too much time on his hands.

NIGHTINGALE raises his coffee mug in salute.

NIGHTINGALE
That's my girl.
(a beat)
Have you still got that friend over at the DSS?

JENNY
(hesitantly)
Yes...

NIGHTINGALE
See if Sebastian Mitchell is still alive, will you.

JENNY looks worried.

NIGHTINGALE
Where's the cheque book?

JENNY
Where it always is.

NIGHTINGALE gives her a sarcastic smile. JENNY gets it from
a filing cabinet.

JENNY
You know we're almost in the red?

NIGHTINGALE
I'm getting the electricity connected at the house.

> JENNY
> You're not going to live there?

> NIGHTINGALE
> It's a mansion, Jenny. What would I do in a mansion?

NIGHTINGALE heads for the door.

> JENNY
> Jack...

NIGHTINGALE looks around. JENNY is clearly concerned.

She shakes her head.

> JENNY
> Forget it.

EXT. GOSLING'S HOUSE - DAY

NIGHTINGALE drives up in front of the house.

INT. HALLWAY, GOSLING'S HOUSE - DAY

NIGHTINGALE opens the door. It's dark and gloomy inside and NIGHTINGALE flicks on the light switch.

Lights come on.

NIGHTINGALE walks towards the dining room.

INT. DINING ROOM, GOSLING'S HOUSE - DAY

NIGHTINGALE opens the secret door in the paneling. He gropes for a light switch and finds it.

INT. BASEMENT, GOSLING's HOUSE - DAY

NIGHTINGALE walks down into the basement.

He goes over to the CCTV monitors. Views of the interior and exterior of the house. Everything is as it should be.

NIGHTINGALE walks around the basement, picking up Black Magic and witchcraft artifacts. There is some weird stuff on display.

He goes over to the shelves of books and runs his fingers along them. Weird titles. 'A History of Sacrifice'. 'Egyptian Immortality'. 'Beasts From Hell'.

NIGHTINGALE takes out Beasts From Hell and flicks through it. There are hellish creatures inside. Dragons. Serpents. Monsters.

As he studies it, a dark figure walks across one of the CCTV screens. NIGHTINGALE doesn't notice.

NIGHTINGALE puts the book back. He goes over to a filing cabinet and pulls it open. It's full of records. Receipts. Bank statements.

NIGHTINGALE pulls out a file and looks at it. As he concentrates on the file, he doesn't notice the figure walk across the CCTV monitors that are covering the dining room. Two monitors showing the figure from different angles.

The lights flicker and the basement is plunged into darkness.

                        NIGHTINGALE
    Shit.

NIGHTINGALE uses his cigarette lighter to light a candle. He heads up the stairs.

As he gets to the top of the stairs, he realises there's a figure standing there. It's ROBBIE HOYLE.

NIGHTINGALE

Hell's bloody bells!

HOYLE

I did knock.

NIGHTINGALE

What the hell are you doing here?

HOYLE

Jenny said you might need help.

INT. KITCHEN, GOSLING'S HOUSE - DAY

NIGHTINGALE is standing at a fuse box. He clicks on a fuse and the lights come back on. HOYLE watches.

NIGHTINGALE

What exactly did she say?

HOYLE

Just that she was worried. Have you looked in a mirror? The state of you. Where did you sleep last night?

NIGHTINGALE

Don't ask.

HOYLE

She just thought that maybe I should have a chat with you.

NIGHTINGALE

About what?

HOYLE

About what you're doing here.

                    NIGHTINGALE
I'm trying to find my mother. My real mother.

INT. BASEMENT, GOSLING'S HOUSE - DAY

The lights are on again.

                    NIGHTINGALE
Assuming that Ainsley Gosling really is my father, he must
know who my birth mother is.

                        HOYLE
Wouldn't adoption records show that?

                    NIGHTINGALE
My birth certificate has my adoptive parents on it.

                        HOYLE
That can't be right.

                    NIGHTINGALE
It could be if it was done without telling the authorities. The
Nightingales were given a newborn baby and they passed it
off as their own.

  NIGHTINGALE waves his arm around the basement.

                    NIGHTINGALE
The answer could be somewhere in here. Gosling kept
records of everything he did. Every penny he spent.
                      (a beat)
Shouldn't you be at work?

                        HOYLE
Late shift.

NIGHTINGALE pulls out several files and hands them to
HOYLE.

                    NIGHTINGALE
You want to make yourself useful?

HOYLE smiles and takes the files.

INT. BASEMENT, GOSLING'S HOUSE- DAY (later)

HOYLE is frowning as he looks through a stack of receipts.

NIGHTINGALE is working his way along a line of books, taking
them out, checking them and putting them back.

                        HOYLE
Have you any idea how much he spent on those books?

                    NIGHTINGALE
A fair whack.

                        HOYLE
He bought a copy of something called the Formicarius for
two million dollars.

                    NIGHTINGALE
What?

                        HOYLE
Some sort of demonology book. He paid a guy in New York
two million dollars for a copy. Published in 1435. But there
are others. Half a million quid. Three hundred thousand.
Those books are where all his money went.

                    NIGHTINGALE
He was trying to find a way out.

                        HOYLE
A way out?

NIGHTINGALE

He'd done the deal, sold my soul in exchange for riches and power. He had a change of heart and tried to renege on the deal.

(off the books)

He thought the answer might lie in these.

HOYLE

You're starting to believe this mumbo jumbo.

NIGHTINGALE

I'm getting inside his head, that's all. I want to know what he was thinking when he killed himself.

HOYLE

Because?

NIGHTINGALE

Because he was my father.

HOYLE

He was your genetic father. You never knew him. And why are we looking for your genetic mother?

NIGHTINGALE shrugs.

HOYLE

You think it might be true, don't you?

NIGHTINGALE

Don't be soppy.

HOYLE

You want to ask her. That's what this is about.

NIGHTINGALE

I don't think he sold my soul. But I think he believed that he did.

(a beat)

Besides, I haven't got a mark.

                          HOYLE
What?

NIGHTINGALE sighs.

                        NIGHTINGALE
They say that if your soul belongs to the devil, you carry a
mark. Like a tattoo.

                          HOYLE
You're starting to scare me, Jack.

                        NIGHTINGALE
A pentangle. But I haven't got a tattoo. I'd know. Hell, you've
seen me in the changing rooms.

                          HOYLE
Not a pretty sight.

                        NIGHTINGALE
But no pentangle. So it's all bollocks.

HOYLE looks down at the file and frowns.

                          HOYLE
When's your birthday?

                        NIGHTINGALE
Next week.

HOYLE picks up a bank statement.

                          HOYLE
Almost thirty-three years ago, he made out a cheque for
twenty grand to a woman called Rebecca Keeley.
                        (a beat)
What do you think?

                        NIGHTINGALE
Worth a try.

INT. NIGHTINGALE'S OFFICE - DAY

NIGHTINGALE walks in with HOYLE. HOYLE is carrying a
stack of files that he's taken from the basement. JENNY is on the
phone.

                         JENNY
     It is in the post, Mr Etchells. I'm not just saying that.
                        (a beat)
     I will. Cross my heart.

JENNY hangs up.

                      NIGHTINGALE
     Did your DSS mate get anywhere with Sebastian Mitchell?

                         JENNY
     I haven't heard back yet.

NIGHTINGALE drops a piece of paper down in front of her.

                      NIGHTINGALE
     Get him to check her as well.

JENNY looks at the piece of paper.

                         JENNY
     Who is she?

                      NIGHTINGALE
     My mother. Maybe.

                         JENNY
     Your real mother?

                      NIGHTINGALE
     Like I said, maybe.

                         JENNY
     Did you see a mirror anywhere. A big mirror?

NIGHTINGALE

What?

JENNY picks up the diary and shows a page to NIGHTINGALE.
There's a sketch of an ornate mirror, the frame composed of
carved snakes and other weird creatures.

NIGHTINGALE
Yeah. Maybe. In the basement. Why?

JENNY
It's a way of talking to the dead.

NIGHTINGALE
Jenny...

JENNY
I'm just telling you what Gosling says, that's all. He used it to
talk to ghosts. Friendly spirits.

INT. NIGHTINGALE'S SITTING ROOM - NIGHT

NIGHTINGALE is sitting on his sofa. He had a home-made
Ouija board on his coffee table - pieces of paper on which he has
written the letters of the alphabet, arranged in a circle.

He is drinking whisky, and smoking.

In the centre of the circle of letters is an upturned glass.

NIGHTINGALE reaches out to touch the glass. Then pulls back
his hand.

NIGHTINGALE
(to himself)
This is stupid.

He paces around the room. He drinks. He smokes. He stares at the letters on the table. He drinks some more. He sits down. He takes another drink and then slowly reaches out to rest the fingers of his right hand on the bottom of the glass.

NIGHTINGALE

Stupid.

The glass slowly begins to move. NIGHTINGALE looks worried. It moves faster, then lurches towards the letter Y.

Then O.

Then U.

Then it pauses. Then it hurtles over to A. Then R. Then E.

Then it pauses. The G. Then O.

NIGHTINGALE roars as he realises what it's spelling out. Her picks up the glass and throws it against the wall. It smashes.

Behind him walks the GIRL, head down, hair over her face, her hands at her side. She almost glides. She moves out of the room, but NIGHTINGALE isn't even aware that she's there.

INT. NIGHTINGALE'S OFFICE - DAY

JENNY is using a mirror to read Mitchell's book and taking notes in a notebook. There's a huge Latin dictionary by her side.

NIGHTINGALE walks in. He looks rough. Unshaven. Tired.

JENNY

You look like shit.

NIGHTINGALE flashes her a tight smile, sits at his desk and pulls out a bottle of whisky.

                      JENNY

You shouldn't be drinking if you're going to visit your mother.

                   NIGHTINGALE

Your DSS mate came through?

                      JENNY

She's in a nursing home.

                   NIGHTINGALE

What about Mitchell?

                      JENNY

No joy yet. He's not on any of the databases. Never paid tax, never been on the electoral role, never seen a doctor. The original invisible man.

NIGHTINGALE puts the whisky back into the drawer.

                      JENNY

And a shave wouldn't hurt.

INT. POLICE STATION - DAY

HOYLE walks through a busy police station. A DRUNK is led to the cells by two UNIFORMED COPS.

HOYLE walks into the CID office.

INT. CID OFFICE - DAY

There's a DETECTIVE working on a terminal.

                   DETECTIVE

Hey, Robbie. Super's been asking for you.

                     HOYLE

Cheers.

HOYLE sits down and opens a file. It's packed with reports and pictures on the AINSLEY GOSLING suicide.

HOYLE flicks through photographs of the crime scene. The body with its horrific head wound. The shotgun.

In the pentangle, HOYLE sees a mobile phone. He looks at the mobile phone.

Then he picks up the phone on his desk and dials.

> HOYLE
> (into phone)
> Good morning, this is Chief Inspector Robbie Hoyle. I need a list of calls made from a mobile phone belonging to Ainsley Gosling. G-O-S-L-I-N-G.

EXT. OLD PEOPLES HOME - DAY

NIGHTINGALE drives up to a residential home.

INT. CORRIDOR, OLD PEOPLE'S HOME - DAY

NIGHTINGALE walks down the corridor with the ADMINISTRATOR. NIGHTINGALE is holding a bunch of flowers.

> ADMINISTRATOR
> I have to say, it was a bolt from the blue when you called. Miss Keeley hasn't had a visitor in the ten years that she's been here.

> NIGHTINGALE
> We lost touch.

They walk past an OLD MAN using a Zimmer frame.

ADMINSTRATOR
And according to her file, no one visited her at her last institution.

NIGHTINGALE
I was adopted. I've only just been told that she's my mother.

ADMINSTRATOR
I hope you don't expect too much from this visit.

EXT. GARDEN, OLD PEOPLE'S HOME - DAY

NIGHTINGALE and the ADMINISTRATOR walk out on to the patio that overlooks the gardens.

Various OLD FOLK are sitting around. Some in wheelchairs. Some connected to drips. Some are being attended to by NURSES.

ADMINSTRATOR
You do realise that for many years your mother was in a mental institution?

NIGHTINGALE
I didn't know that.

ADMINSTRATOR
Frankly, the only reason she came here was because there was no medical treatment suitable and she was no longer considered a danger.

They start to walk together across the garden.

NIGHTINGALE
A danger? To who?

ADMINSTRATOR
To herself. To the staff. Other patients. Not now, of course.

NIGHTINGALE

Why not now?

ADMINSTRATOR

She's fairly infirm these days.

NIGHTINGALE

How old is she?

ADMINSTRATOR

Fifty four. But she looks older. The drugs can have that
effect.

NIGHTINGALE

Drugs?

ADMINSTRATOR

She's had a lifetime of tranquilizers, anti-depressants and
anti-schizophrenia medication.

Ahead of them is an old lady sitting on a bench, staring off into
the distance. She looks about eighty years old.

NIGHTINGALE

You said she was fifty-four?

ADMINSTRATOR

That's right.

NIGHTINGALE

How long has she been institutionalised?

ADMINSTRATOR

More than thirty years.

NIGHTINGALE's face goes tight as he realises the significance
of what she's said. Since he was born.

The ADMINSTRATOR walks up in front of the old woman.

ADMINSTRATOR
Miss Keeley. You have a visitor.

There's a blank look on MISS KEELEY's face. No reaction.

ADMINSTRATOR
It's your son. Jack.

MISS KEELEY frowns.

The ADMINISTRATOR smiles brightly.

ADMINSTRATOR
Well, I'll leave you two alone.

As the ADMINISTRATOR walks back to the house,
NIGHTINGALE smiles at MISS KEELEY. He holds out the
flowers.

NIGHTINGALE
Must be a bit of a surprise, me turning up like this.

MISS KEELEY takes the flowers. She looks confused.

MISS KEELEY
Who are you?

NIGHTINGALE
Jack. Jack Nightingale.

MISS KEELEY
I don't know you.
(a beat)
Do I?

NIGHTINGALE sits down next to her.

NIGHTINGALE
Do you know Ainsley Gosling?

MISS KEELEY shudders. She shakes her head.

NIGHTINGALE
You do know him. Don't you?

MISS KEELEY
I don't want to talk about him. I don't want to talk to you.

NIGHTINGALE
He's my father.

MISS KEELEY stares at him for a long time. Then she slowly crosses herself. She has a small crucifix around her neck and she kisses it.

MISS KEELEY
My God...

NIGHTINGALE
He paid you to have a child, didn't he?

MISS KEELEY
How do you....

She leaves the sentence unfinished.

NIGHTINGALE
Twenty thousand pounds.

MISS KEELEY
You don't understand.

NIGHTINGALE
I want to. That's why I'm here.

INT. CID OFFICE - DAY

HOYLE is on his computer. An email arrives. A list of calls.

He looks down the list of calls. There are a dozen calls to the same number.

HOYLE looks at the date. April 15.

Then he goes through the file and looks for the date that
GOSLING died. April 15.

HOYLE smiles at the date on the list of phone calls. April 15.

INT. CID OFFICE - LATER

HOYLE is on the phone.

> HOYLE
> (into phone)
> That's right. It's a landline.
> (a beat)
> Sebastian Mitchell? I'm going to need the address.

HOYLE listens and writes an address on his notepad.

INT. GARDEN, OLD PEOPLE'S HOME - DAY

NIGHTINGALE continues to talk to MISS KEELEY.

> NIGHTINGALE
> Why? Why did you do it?

> MISS KEELEY
> You know what he's like. How persuasive he can be.

> NIGHTINGALE
> I never met him. And he's dead now.

> MISS KEELEY
> Dead?

> NIGHTINGALE
> Last week.

                         MISS KEELEY
How?

                         NIGHTINGALE
He killed himself.

For the first time, MISS KEELEY smiles.

                         MISS KEELEY
    Good riddance. I hope he rots in hell.

EXT. POLICE STATION - DAY

HOYLE walks out of the police station, a file under his arm. He
takes out his mobile phone and calls NIGHTINGALE's number
as he walks down the street.

EXT. GARDEN, OLD PEOPLES HOME - DAY

NIGHTINGALE's phone starts to ring and he takes it out. He
sees that it's HOYLE calling but he doesn't want to talk to him
while MISS KEELEY is talking.

NIGHTINGALE presses the 'NO' button to refuse the call.

EXT. STREET - DAY

HOYLE starts to cross the road, looking both ways. It's busy,
there's quite a bit of traffic, but he sees a gap and goes for it.

HOYLE is talking to NIGHTINGALE's answerphone.

                         HOYLE
    Jack, it's Robbie. Look, I think I might have found what
    you're looking for. Give me a call back, yeah?

                         PROSERPINE
Hey, Mister!

HOYLE stops at the shout. He stands in the middle of the road, still holding his phone.

PROSERPINE is standing at the roadside, dressed all in black, her COLLIE on its lead.

> PROSERPINE
>
> Got a cigarette?

HOYLE opens his mouth to speak.

> HOYLE
>
> Sorry, I don't...

BANG! HOYLE is hit by a black van. Killed instantly.

PROSERPINE smiles.

> PROSERPINE
>
> Never mind.

The file lies in the road. The wind picks up and blows the contents away.

EXT. GARDEN, OLD PEOPLES HOME - DAY

NIGHTINGALE carries on talking to MISS KEELEY.

> NIGHTINGALE
>
> How did you meet him?

> MISS KEELEY
>
> At a party. We were playing with a Ouija board. Talking to spirits. It was a joke. A game. Until he joined in. Then it stopped being a game. We started to get messages.

MISS KEELEY shudders.

NIGHTINGALE

It's a con. Somebody always cheats.

MISS KEELEY

Not when he was there. There was no faking the messages
we got.

NIGHTINGALE

He paid you to have a child, didn't he?

MISS KEELEY

It wasn't like that.

NIGHTINGALE

I've seen his accounts. He paid you twenty thousand pounds.
And you gave him what he wanted. A child.

MISS KEELEY

I wanted a child because I loved him. Because I thought I
loved him. It was only when I fell pregnant that he told me
what he planned to do.

MISS KEELEY starts to frown.

MISS KEELEY

How old are you?

NIGHTINGALE

Thirty-two.
                    (a beat)
I'm thirty-three next week.

MISS KEELEY gropes for a crucifix around her neck.

MISS KEELEY

My God...

NIGHTINGALE

How could you? How could you give me away like that?
Didn't I mean anything to you?

> MISS KEELEY

I didn't give you away. I never even held you. He took you from me.

> NIGHTINGALE

I was your child!

> MISS KEELEY

You don't understand.

> NIGHTINGALE

No. I don't.

MISS KEELEY kisses her crucifix.

INT. NIGHTINGALE'S OFFICE - DAY

NIGHTINGALE walks into the office. JENNY is already at her desk. There's a cup of coffee on her desk and NIGHTINGALE picks it up as he walks by.

> JENNY

Hey, that's mine!

> NIGHTINGALE

I need the caffeine, sorry.

> JENNY

Jack!

> NIGHTINGALE

I've had a shitty morning.

> JENNY

Your mum?

> NIGHTINGALE

It was weird.

                              JENNY
Was she surprised to see you?

                           NIGHTINGALE
Horrified, more like.

NIGHTINGALE sits down at his desk and takes out his bottle of
whisky. He pours a big slug into his coffee.

                           NIGHTINGALE
I'm her son, no question. But the day I was born, Gosling
took me away.

                              JENNY
What about now? Does she want to... you know... form some
sort of relationship with you?

NIGHTINGALE shakes his head.

                              JENNY
I'm sorry, Jack.

The office door opens. Two men are there. Plainclothes
DETECTIVES. INSPECTOR DAN EVANS and DC NEIL
DERBYSHIRE.

                              EVANS
Jack Nightingale?

                           NIGHTINGALE
That's what it says on the door.

                              EVANS
I'm Inspector Dan Evans. This is DC Neil Derbyshire.

                           NIGHTINGALE
Is this about my drunk driving?

                              EVANS
Drunk driving?

NIGHTINGALE
I'll be pleading guilty. There's no need for an interview.

EVANS
Do you know Chief Inspector Robbie Hoyle?

NIGHTINGALE
(wary)
Yes.

EVANS
In what capacity?

NIGHTINGALE
He's a friend. I used to work with him. What's happened?

EVANS
He's dead.

NIGHTINGALE
What?

EVANS
RTA this morning.

NIGHTINGALE
Shit. No. Shit.

NIGHTINGALE shakes his head. JENNY is shocked,

NIGHTINGALE
Shit.

DERBYSHIRE
We got your number off his mobile. He called you just before...

NIGHTINGALE
What happened?

DERBYSHIRE

He was hit by a van. Crossing the road.

NIGHTINGALE lights a cigarette.

EVANS

Stupid accident. One of those things.

NIGHTINGALE

Had the driver been drinking?

EVANS

Stone cold sober. Says that Hoyle wasn't looking where he was going. Stepped out in front of him.

NIGHTINGALE

Oh God. Anna. His wife. Has anyone told his wife?

EVANS

His boss is around there now.

NIGHTINGALE

Chalmers?

EVANS nods.

NIGHTINGALE

She hates Chalmers.

EVANS

You used to work for hostage negotiation, didn't you?

NIGHTINGALE

In another life.

DERBYSHIRE

You're the one that killed that paedophile, right? The banker that was molesting his daughter?

NIGHTINGALE
I was there when he died.

DERBYSHIRE
They said you threw him out of a ten storey window.

NIGHTINGALE
They?

DERBYSHIRE
Hey, I'd have done the same in your place.

DERBYSHIRE looks across at EVANS.

EVANS
Most of us would, if we had the balls.

DERBYSHIRE nods.

EVANS
I'm a dad myself. Two girls. If anyone touched them...

NIGHTINGALE
Is there anything else?

EVAN can see that he's touched a nerve.

EVANS
We're just clearing up loose ends.

NIGHTINGALE
But there's nothing...untoward?

EVANS
You think there might be?

NIGHTINGALE pulls a face and shakes his head.

EVANS
Was he doing something for you? A bit of work on the side?

NIGHTINGALE

No. Robbie was too straight for that.

EVANS gives NIGHTINGALE a final look, then the two DETECTIVES leave.

NIGHTINGALE looks at JENNY.

NIGHTINGALE

I need a drink.

JENNY

Me too.

INT. DINING ROOM, OLD PEOPLE'S HOME - EVENING

MISS KEELEY is sitting at a dining table. A West Indian CARE ASSISTANT is cutting up her boiled chicken with a knife and feeding her.

MISS KEELEY's face is totally blank.

CARE ASSISTANT

Well, that was nice, wasn't it? You son coming to see you. What a lovely surprise that must have been? You must have had so much to talk about.

No reaction from MISS KEELEY. The CARE ASSISTANT puts the knife down.

MISS KEELEY looks down at the knife.

The CARE ASSISTANT walks out.

EXT. LONDON STREET - DAY

JENNY and NIGHTINGALE are walking towards a pub.

NIGHTINGALE

I don't believe this. I was with him yesterday.

NIGHTINGALE takes out his phone.

NIGHTINGALE

That cop said Robbie phoned me.

NIGHTINGALE picks up the message that HOYLE left.

HOYLE
(on phone)

Jack, it's Robbie. Look, I think I might have found what you're looking for. Give me a call back, yeah?

NIGHTINGALE flinches as he hears what happens next.

PROSERPINE
(on phone)

Hey, Mister!

(a beat)

Got a cigarette?

HOYLE
(on phone)

Sorry, I don't...

NIGHTINGALE stares at his phone in horror.

JENNY

What?

INT. PUBLIC HOUSE - DAY

NIGHTINGALE takes a long drink of whisky. JENNY sips a white wine.

NIGHTINGALE

I can't believe it.

There's nothing JENNY can say.

> NIGHTINGALE
>
> Shit. I've known him for almost twelve years. We were at
> Hendon together.

> JENNY
>
> He was a good guy.

> NIGHTINGALE
>
> He was a better cop than me.
>> (a beat)
> Anna's going to be wrecked.

NIGHTINGALE drains his glass and waves for another round of
drinks.

> JENNY
>
> Not for me.

NIGHTINGALE gives her a warning look - he doesn't want her
to tell him that he's drinking too much, too early. She shrugs.

> NIGHTINGALE
>
> He was on the phone to me when he died. Maybe if he hadn't
> been on the phone...

> JENNY
>
> It was an accident, they said.

> NIGHTINGALE
>
> I know. It's just... Shit.

NIGHTINGALE shakes his head.

> NIGHTINGALE
>
> Shit, shit, shit.

> JENNY
>
> At least it was quick.

NIGHTINGALE

That's bollocks.

JENNY looks hurt. NIGHTINGALE tries to explain.

NIGHTINGALE

They always say that. At least he didn't suffer. At least it was quick. It's bollocks. One moment they're there, then they're gone. Bang. Thank you and good night.

JENNY

But isn't that better than getting sick and lying in a hospital bed wired up to a life support machine?

NIGHTINGALE

Too much unfinished business. There's no time to prepare yourself. To prepare others.

NIGHTINGALE takes a drink from his glass.

NIGHTINGALE

Sudden death just rips people away. It leaves too many unanswered questions.

NIGHTINGALE drains his glass and waves for another from the BARMAN.

JENNY

Jack...

JENNY puts a hand on his arm but he shrugs her off.

JENNY

That's not going to help.

NIGHTINGALE

What is?

EXT. GOSLING's HOUSE - NIGHT

JENNY and NIGHTINGALE get out of JENNY's car and stand looking at the house.

INT. BASEMENT, GOSLING's house - NIGHT

NIGHTINGALE and JENNY walk along the aisles looking at the artifacts.

> NIGHTINGALE
> It was here somewhere.

They find the mirror. It's big and looks evil.

INT. BEDROOM, GOSLING'S HOUSE - NIGHT, later

They've carried the mirror up to the bedroom and put it against a wall. Around it are candles, which JENNY is lighting.

> JENNY
> The book says it has to be candle light.

> NIGHTINGALE
> You believe this?

> JENNY
> Your father did.

She lights the last candle.

> JENNY
> The lights.

> NIGHTINGALE
> What?

> JENNY
> Switch the lights off.

NIGHTINGALE switches off the light. The bedroom looks a lot scarier in the candle light.

NIGHTINGALE walks over to stand next to JENNY.

>   NIGHTINGALE
> Now what?

>   JENNY
> We look in the mirror.

The two of them look at their reflections.

>   NIGHTINGALE
> This is stupid.

>   JENNY
> Just give it a go.

>   NIGHTINGALE
> And you think Robbie will come and talk to us?

>   JENNY
> Gosling says that it's a way for friendly spirits to talk to the living.

>   NIGHTINGALE
> Yeah, well the only friendly spirits I have any faith in are Johnnie Walker and Jack Daniels.

>   JENNY
> Jack...

>   NIGHTINGALE
> Okay, okay.

NIGHTINGALE stares at his reflection. So does JENNY. Behind them, just darkness.

JENNY
Whatever happens, you must only look in the mirror.

NIGHTINGALE pulls a scornful face.

JENNY
I'm just telling you what it says in the diary.

They stare into the mirror.

NIGHTINGALE
(in a spooky voice)
Is there anybody there?

No reply. They continue to stare at the mirror. Then they see something. A blur. Getting closer. Slowly.

NIGHTINGALE
Can you see that?

JENNY
Shhhh.

The blur becomes a figure. It's the GIRL, dressed in a long white dress, her hands hanging limply at her sides, her head down so that her blonde curly hair is covering her face.

The GIRL moves slowly. Sometimes she flickers like a badly-received TV signal.

NIGHTINGALE turns to look over his shoulder.

JENNY
No!

She puts a hand on his shoulder and makes him face the mirror.

The GIRL gets closer. In the reflection she's standing between NIGHTINGALE and JENNY.

Slowly, the girl raises her head. It's SOPHIE. Her face is a deathly white, there are dark patches under her eyes. She looks very, very sad.

> NIGHTINGALE
>
> Sophie?

> SOPHIE
>
> I'm scared.

> JENNY
>
> You know her?

NIGHTINGALE ignores JENNY. He's staring at the reflection. At SOPHIE.

SOPHIE stares intently at NIGHTINGALE.

> SOPHIE
>
> She's coming for you, Jack.

> NIGHTINGALE
>
> Who? Who's coming for me?

> SOPHIE
>
> She wants your soul. She says I mustn't talk to you. She says bad things will happen to me if I talk to you.

SOPHIE flickers. Then her image hardens.

> NIGHTINGALE
>
> Do you know where you are, Sophie?

SOPHIE shudders and looks around.

> SOPHIE
>
> It's cold. And dark. I wanted my Jessica but she says I can't have anything here.

SOPHIE looks suddenly scared.

SOPHIE

She's coming. I have to go.

SOPHIE turns to walk away.

NIGHTINGALE turns to look behind him.

JENNY

Jack! No!

CRACK! The mirror shatters into a thousand shards. As the shards spin through the air in slow motion, images of PROSERPINE are reflected in the glass.

NIGHTINGALE looks around the room. There's no sign of SOPHIE.

INT. MISS KEELEY'S ROOM - NIGHT

MISS KEELEY is lying in bed.

A NURSE is leaving.

NURSE

Good night. God bless.

MISS KEELEY closes her eyes.

MISS KEELEY

Good night.

The NURSE switches the light off and leaves.

MISS KEELEY sits up and switches on a lamp on her side table.

From under the bedclothes she takes out a knife from the dining room.

> MISS KEELEY
> (to herself)

God bless.

MISS KEELEY starts to hack away at her wrist with the knife.

INT. NIGHTINGALE'S FLAT - NIGHT

NIGHTINGALE sits on his sofa, smoking, drinking whisky and looking through old photographs of when he was training to be a policeman.

In several of the photographs he's standing next to a younger HOYLE.

> NIGHTINGALE
> (to himself)
> Shit, Robbie. Shit, shit, shit.

JENNY walks in, holding a tray with two coffee mugs on it.

JENNY gives him a half smile, there's nothing she can say to ease his pain.

> JENNY

There's no sugar.

> NIGHTINGALE

I don't take sugar.

Then NIGHTINGALE realises what she meant - JENNY does take sugar in her coffee.

> NIGHTINGALE

Sorry.

> JENNY
> Your self-centeredness is just one of your many attractive qualities.

She sits down next to him on the sofa.

                    JENNY
It could all be...I don't know, a hallucination.

                    NIGHTINGALE
What, we both imagined the same thing? And what about
Robbie? What happened to him wasn't a bad dream. I'm
fucked, Jenny. With a capital F.

                    JENNY
Jack...

NIGHTINGALE sits back on the sofa. He looks wrecked.
JENNY moves to kiss him.

At first NIGHTINGALE responds, but then he pushes her away.

                    NIGHTINGALE
I'm sorry.

                    JENNY
                  (confused)
For what?

                    NIGHTINGALE
I can't. I just can't.

                    JENNY
Let me stay with you tonight. I'll just lie with you. We don't
have to do anything.

                    NIGHTINGALE
It's not that.

                    JENNY
What is it then?

NIGHTINGALE takes a deep breath.

NIGHTINGALE
It's stupid.

JENNY
What's stupid? You must know how I feel about you.

NIGHTINGALE
Jenny...

JENNY
Don't 'Jenny' me. I hate it when you 'Jenny' me.

JENNY looks upset.

JENNY
I don't understand you.

NIGHTINGALE is fighting with himself. He wants to open up,
but it's hard. Maybe impossible.

NIGHTINGALE
Everyone who has ever gotten close to me has died.

JENNY
That's ridiculous.

NIGHTINGALE
It's true.

JENNY
(off the picture)
Robbie's death was...

NIGHTINGALE
What? An accident? And my parents?

JENNY
A car accident.

                    NIGHTINGALE
Sophie?

                       JENNY
She killed herself. Because her father was raping her. Jack,
everyone knows people who have died. Everyone dies. It's
part of life. You just have to make the best of your time here.

                    NIGHTINGALE
There's more than that to it, Jenny.

NIGHTINGALE sighs. He runs his hands through his hair. Fights
with himself.

                    NIGHTINGALE
There was a girl at university. My first real girlfriend. Way
back when.

INT. STUDENT BATHROOM - DAY

The shower curtain is drawn. Water is dripping.

                 NIGHTINGALE (V.O.)
If things had worked out differently, maybe we'd have ended
up together.

The camera moves slowly towards the shower curtain.

                 NIGHTINGALE (V.O.)
She was perfect for me.

The camera moves around the shower curtain. Lying in the bath,
covered in blood, with a razor blade in one hand, is a PRETTY
BRUNETTE, eighteen years old.

                 NIGHTINGALE (V.O.)
Until she killed herself.

INT. NIGHTINGALE'S FLAT - NIGHT

NIGHTINGALE looks shattered. Defeated.

> NIGHTINGALE
> Like I said, everyone who has ever got close to me, really close, has died.

> JENNY
> And what? You think the devil is responsible for that? That's such a crock of shit, Jack Nightingale. I've heard some crappy excuses for not wanting to make a commitment but that takes the biscuit, it really does.

> NIGHTINGALE
> Jenny...

> JENNY
> Don't 'Jenny' me. I told you, don't 'Jenny' me.

JENNY stands up.

> JENNY
> Ask me to stay, Jack.

They look at each other for a long time. NIGHTINGALE wants to, but he can't.

JENNY storms over to the front door and yanks it open,

> JENNY
> Go to hell.

She slams the door.

> NIGHTINGALE
> (to himself)
> I think that's a given.

EXT. LONDON BACK STREET - DAY

NIGHTINGALE walks down a quiet street lined with small, old-fashioned shops. He's holding a carrier bag containing four books from the basement in Gosling's house.

He finds the shop he's looking for. It's an old book shop which also sells New Age stuff - crystals, pendants, Tarot cards.

INT. BOOK SHOP - DAY

There's a old lady behind the counter, serving two PRETTY TEENAGERS. MRS STEADMAN is tiny and birdlike with mischievous eyes. The PRETTY TEENAGERS are dressed in black and have lots of body piercings. MRS STEADMAN hands one of the TEENAGERS a small bag.

                    MRS STEADMAN
    Use it sparingly, mind. A little goes a long way.

The PRETTY TEENAGERS giggle as they leave.

MRS STEADMAN smiles at NIGHTINGALE.

                    MRS STEADMAN
    How can I help you?

                    NIGHTINGALE
    Do you buy second-hand books?

                    MRS STEADMAN
    Not really. Not unless they were special.

NIGHTINGALE takes out the four books from his carrier bag and gives them to her.

MRS STEADMAN examines the books. She looks horrified and starts shaking her head. She thrusts them back at NIGHTINGALE.

> MRS STEADMAN

No.

> NIGHTINGALE

But they're valuable, right?

> MRS STEADMAN

Get out of my shop.

> NIGHTINGALE

I just want to sell them, that's all.

> MRS STEADMAN
> (screaming)

GET OUT OF MY SHOP!!

NIGHTINGALE backs away, horrified.

EXT. LONDON BACK STREET - NIGHT

MRS STEADMAN lets herself out of the shop. She locks the
door. As she locks it, she senses that there is someone behind her.
She whirls around but there is no one there.

EXT. DARK STREET- NIGHT

MRS STEADMAN walks along a deserted street, her feet
clicking on the footpath.

She stops. Did she hear something? She looks around. It's dark.

EXT. ENTRANCE TO ALLEY - NIGHT

MRS STEADMAN has to walk down an alley to get to her home.
It's dark and she hesitates.

Then she starts to walk. Slowly. Then more quickly.

Then she stops and listens.

A light flickers. A cigarette lighter. It's NIGHTINGALE in the shadows.

> NIGHTINGALE
> We have to talk.

INT. MRS STEADMAN'S HOUSE - NIGHT

MRS STEADMAN pours tea from a teapot into a cup. The books are on the table.

> MRS STEADMAN
> Not too strong for you?

> NIGHTINGALE
> It's fine.
> (off the books)
> So they are valuable?

> MRS STEADMAN
> To the right people, yes. But the right people are the wrong people, if you see what I mean.

She picks up one of the books.

> MRS STEADMAN
> This one I'd happily buy. But the rest are...

She frowns, wondering what the right word is.

> NIGHTINGALE
> Evil?

> MRS STEADMAN
> Worse than evil.

> NIGHTINGALE
> That's why you threw me out of the shop?

> MRS STEADMAN
You don't understand how dangerous they can be.

NIGHTINGALE holds up his cigarettes.

> NIGHTINGALE
Do you mind?

> MRS STEADMAN
I'd rather you didn't.

She pats her chest.

> MRS STEADMAN
Asthma.

NIGHTINGALE puts the cigarettes away.

> NIGHTINGALE
So you believe in this stuff do you? Magic and that.

> MRS STEADMAN
It's not a question of belief. It's whether or not it works.

> NIGHTINGALE
And does it work?

MRS STEADMAN chuckles.

> MRS STEADMAN
Oh yes, young man. It works.

> NIGHTINGALE
Black magic? Spells? Curses?

> MRS STEADMAN
There's no such thing as black magic. Or white magic. Just magic.

> NIGHTINGALE
But I thought...(that there was...)

MRS STEADMAN shakes her finger at him.

> MRS STEADMAN
> It's like electricity, young man. You can use it to power a life
> support machine, or an electric chair. Electricity itself isn't
> good or bad. Black or white.

> NIGHTINGALE
> But stuff like selling your soul to the devil. That's possible?

> MRS STEADMAN
> That's easy. You go to a churchyard at midnight and draw a
> magic circle. Within the circle draw two crosses on the
> ground. Take a handful of wormwood in each hand, and the
> Bible under your left arm. Toss the wormwood in your right
> hand down and the left handful up. Then say the Lord's
> Prayer backward.

> NIGHTINGALE
> And that's it?

> MRS STEADMAN
> That's it. On your way home, leave the Bible on the steps of
> a church.

NIGHTINGALE frowns. He expected more than that.

> NIGHTINGALE
> And what about breaking a pact with the devil?

> MRS STEADMAN
> You renounce him. Three times.

> NIGHTINGALE
> That's it?

> MRS STEADMAN
> You expected something more dramatic?

NIGHTINGALE reaches for his cigarettes again but then remembers that MRS STEADMAN doesn't like smoke.

NIGHTINGALE
I thought there were contracts. Signed in blood.

MRS STEADMAN
Ah....

NIGHTINGALE
So there is more.

MRS STEADMAN
You were asking about making a pact with THE devil. Contracts with minor devils are a more complicated matter. There are 66 princes under the devil, each with 6,666 legions.

NIGHTINGALE
And each legion has 6,666 devils.

MRS STEADMAN
Exactly. And each has its own way of doing business. I'd steer clear of such things, young man.

NIGHTINGALE
But there are ways of selling a soul, right?

MRS STEADMAN
In theory. You have to renounce God and the Church. You pay homage to The Devil, drink the blood of sacrificed children, and strike your deal. A contract is drawn up and signed with blood drawn from the left arm. Then your name is inscribed in the 'red book' of death.

NIGHTINGALE
Have you ever heard of a man called Sebastian Mitchell?

MRS STEADMAN looks apprehensive.

                    MRS STEADMAN
He was your father?

                    NIGHTINGALE
No. But I have one of his books.

                    MRS STEADMAN
Burn it. Burn all of them.

INT. NIGHTINGALE'S OFFICE - DAY

NIGHTINGALE walks in and drops an envelope on JENNY's desk.

She opens it. A thousand pounds.

                    JENNY
Who did you kill?

                    NIGHTINGALE
I sold one of the books.

                    JENNY
For a grand?

                    NIGHTINGALE
That was just for one. Should keep the wolf from the door. Apparently if I advertise in Satanist's Weekly I can sell the rest.

                    JENNY
So you're not interested in Sebastian Mitchell any more?

                    NIGHTINGALE
Why?

JENNY hands him a slip of paper.

                    JENNY
My friend in DSS tracked him down.

INT. NIGHTINGALE'S CAR - DAY

NIGHTINGALE drives up to a set of imposing gates set in a high wall. The wall surrounds Mitchell's house.

There's an intercom set into the wall with a camera above it.

NIGHTINGALE presses the intercom.

There's static, but no one speaks.

> NIGHTINGALE
> (into intercom)
> Hello?

No reply.

> NIGHTINGALE
> I'm here to see Mr Mitchell.

Still no reply.

> NIGHTINGALE
> Hello?

NIGHTINGALE presses the intercom button again.

A woman's voice is on the intercom.

> INTERCOM
> Mr Mitchell doesn't see visitors.

> NIGHTINGALE
> Can you tell him it's about his book.

> INTERCOM
> Mr Mitchell doesn't see visitors. If you don't go away, the police will be called.

> NIGHTINGALE
> Tell him my father was Ainsley Gosling.

Silence.

> NIGHTINGALE
>
> Hello?

> INTERCOM
>
> Get out of the car and face the intercom.

EXT. GATES, MITCHELL'S HOUSE - DAY

NIGHTINGALE faces the intercom.

> INTERCOM
>
> Place your face close to the camera. Look into the lens and
> do not blink.

NIGHTINGALE does as he's told.

A red light passes over NIGHTINGALE's eyes. A retinal
scanner.

After the scanner has finished, NIGHTINGALE frowns,
wondering what the hell is going on.

Then the gate buzzes and opens.

EXT. MITCHELL'S HOUSE - DAY

NIGHTINGALE gets out of his car in front of a huge modern
house, all white walls and glass.

The house is covered with CCTV cameras.

A SEVERE WOMAN opens the front door.

> SEVERE WOMAN
>
> You are...?

NIGHTINGALE
Jack Nightingale.

SEVERE WOMAN
Do you have any identification?

NIGHTINGALE gives her his business card. She looks at it.

She steps aside to let him in.

INT. HALLWAY. MITCHELL'S HOUSE- DAY

The hallway is huge and full of light. There are more CCTV cameras.

On the walls, modern art. It has the feel of an upmarket gallery.

Two men in black suits appear. They are holding handguns. They keep their distance but watch NIGHTINGALE closely.

SEVERE WOMAN
There are certain house rules that have to be followed.

NIGHTINGALE
Okay.

SEVERE WOMAN
You will see that Mr Mitchell is within a circle. You must not get within six feet of the perimeter of the circle.

NIGHTINGALE
Okay.

SEVERE WOMAN
You must make no move to touch Mr Mitchell. Or to give him anything. My associates are here to ensure that the rules are not broken. They will use whatever force is necessary.

NIGHTINGALE looks at the guns. He nods.

INT. MAIN ROOM, MITCHELL'S HOUSE - DAY

The SEVERE WOMAN takes NIGHTINGALE through to the main room. It's huge, all white walls and glass, and bare floorboards. The room is covered by CCTV cameras.

The two armed men follow them into the room and stand at either side, guns in hand.

One wall of the room is all glass, overlooking an immaculate lawn.

MITCHELL is sitting in a wing-backed antique chair, looking out over the garden. He's almost ninety years old and has an oxygen mask over his face. There's an oxygen cylinder next to him.

Around the chair is a protective circle and pentagram. At each point of the pentagram there's a black candle.

MITCHELL takes the oxygen mask away from his face. He wheezes as he talks.

> MITCHELL
>
> Gosling sent you?

> NIGHTINGALE
>
> He's dead.

> MITCHELL
>
> How? Specifically

> .NIGHTINGALE
>
> Suicide?

> MITCHELL
>
> How?

> NIGHTINGALE
>
> Shotgun to the head.

MITCHELL laughs, but the laugh degenerates into a cough and he takes several deep breaths from his oxygen mask.

> MITCHELL
>
> You're his son?

NIGHTINGALE nods and MITCHELL laughs.

> MITCHELL
>
> How old are you?

> NIGHTINGALE
>
> I get asked that a lot these days.
> (a beat)
> Thirty-three next week.

> MITCHELL
>
> He was trying to get out of the deal, you know that?

> NIGHTINGALE
>
> I figured as much. But I don't know why.

> MITCHELL
>
> Guilt, pure and simple. He didn't have what it takes to wield absolute power. He thought that he did, but he was fooling himself.

> NIGHTINGALE
>
> But you do?

> MITCHELL
>
> Oh yes. I do.
> (a beat)
> You read my book?

> NIGHTINGALE
>
> Yes.

> MITCHELL
>
> You read Latin?

NIGHTINGALE

A friend helped me.

MITCHELL

So you know what lies ahead?

NIGHTINGALE

I said I read it. I didn't say I believed it.

MITCHELL

It doesn't matter if you believe it or not.

NIGHTINGALE

I thought it was a matter of faith.

MITCHELL

Faith has nothing to do with it. A deal is a deal. And if your
father followed the instructions in the book, there's no way
out for you.

NIGHTINGALE

My soul for riches and power?

MITCHELL

I don't know what Gosling asked for. But whatever it was, he
regretted it. Eventually.

NIGHTINGALE

He came to see you?

MITCHELL

Several times. He knew I'd done a deal myself. He bought
my library. Most of it. I told him he was wasting his time.
Eventually I refused to allow him in. Then he started
phoning.

NIGHTINGALE
(off the circle)

What's this about?

MITCHELL

Protection.

NIGHTINGALE

From what?

MITCHELL chuckles and then takes more oxygen.

NIGHTINGALE

So you're hiding, too?

MITCHELL

I'm not hiding. She knows where I am. But so long as I'm within the circle, she can't get to me.

NIGHTINGALE

She?

MITCHELL

Proserpine.

NIGHTINGALE

The devil?

MITCHELL

A devil. One of the legion.

NIGHTINGALE

And she's after you.

MITCHELL

Oh yes.

NIGHTINGALE
(off the circle)
So you stay there forever, is that the plan?

MITCHELL coughs and takes more oxygen.

MITCHELL

Cancer. A few months at most. Then I walk into hell of my own accord.

NIGHTINGALE

So you're damned whatever happens?

MITCHELL chuckles.

MITCHELL

It's one thing to be dragged kicking and screaming into the eternal fire. If I walk in under my own steam, I take my place among the princes of hell.

NIGHTINGALE

What if I do the same? What if I stay within a circle?

MITCHELL

It wouldn't help. Your soul is hers. It was sold to Proserpine before you were born.

NIGHTINGALE

In your book, you said there should be a mark?

MITCHELL

A pentangle, yes.

NIGHTINGALE

I don't have a mark.

MITCHELL

If your father sold your soul, you do. You just haven't found it yet.

NIGHTINGALE

And if there's no mark?

MITCHELL

Then you've got nothing to worry about.

MITCHELL starts to laugh. Then cough. Then gasp at his oxygen mask.

INT. HALLWAY, MITCHELL'S HOUSE - DAY

The SEVERE WOMAN escorts NIGHTINGALE towards the exit.

> SEVERE WOMAN
> There's something you should see.

She leads him through an unmarked door.

INT. SECURITY ROOM, MITCHELL'S HOUSE - DAY

The security room has two UNIFORMED SECURITY MEN watching computer screens showing views from the cameras around the Mitchell house. On one wall is a huge map of the area. It's all high-tech.

> SEVERE WOMAN
> You know what a retinal scan is?

> NIGHTINGALE
> Sure.

She nods at a computer screen. NIGHTINGALE peers at it, wondering what he's supposed to be looking at.

It's a retinal scan. Two eyes.

> SEVERE WOMAN
> The left one.

NIGHTINGALE peers closely at the retinal scan on the left. His left eye. He peers closer. Then he sees it. A pentangle.

He looks at the SEVERE WOMAN in horror.

INT. NIGHTINGALE'S BATHROOM - NIGHT

NIGHTINGALE showers. There is a full length mirror on one of the walls.

He gets out of the shower and towels himself dry as he looks at himself in the mirror.

He peers at his reflection in the mirror, trying to stare into his left eye. Impossible, of course. But he can't stop himself from trying.

He has a shaving mirror and he uses it in conjunction with the big bathroom mirror but that doesn't work either. Reflections in reflections.

As he moves the mirror around he catches a glimpse of a face behind him. PROSERPINE, grinning with malice.

                    PROSERPINE
     You're going straight...(to hell, Nightingale)

NIGHTINGALE whirls around. He's alone in the bathroom. He stands staring at his reflection in the full-length mirror. He looks a mess. Haggard. Tired. Scared.

INT. NIGHTINGALE'S SITTING ROOM - NIGHT

NIGHTINGALE sits alone, smoking and drinking whisky. And considering his options.

INT. JENNY'S SITTING ROOM - NIGHT

JENNY's flat is plush. She has family money, a lot of it.

She has just finished rolling a joint. She lights it and inhales. She settles back on her sofa. The phone rings. She sighs and answers it.

JENNY
(into phone))
For God's sake. It's almost midnight.

EXT. GOSLING'S HOUSE - NIGHT

JENNY drives up to the house.

NIGHTINGALE's car is already parked outside.

INT. HALLWAY, GOSLING'S HOUSE - NIGHT

JENNY pushes open the front door.

JENNY's carrying Mitchell's diary and the notebook she has used for the translation.

JENNY
Jack?

No answer. She hears a brushing sound from the dining room. JENNY walks to the dining room.

INT. DINING ROOM, GOSLING'S HOUSE - NIGHT

NIGHTINGALE is brushing the wooden floor clean. He looks scared.

JENNY
What's going on, Jack?

NIGHTINGALE
I spoke to Mitchell.

JENNY
And?

NIGHTINGALE

And it's true. The whole thing, it's true. My father sold my soul. He made a deal with a devil.

JENNY

There's no mark on you, remember?

NIGHTINGALE gives her a sarcastic smile. JENNY realises that he's found a mark.

JENNY

You're joking.

NIGHTINGALE

I wish I was.

JENNY

Where?

NIGHTINGALE

I spy, with my little eye.

JENNY

What do you mean?

NIGHTINGALE points to his left eye.

NIGHTINGALE

My retina.

JENNY

No way.

NIGHTINGALE shrugs and continues to brush the floor.

JENNY
(off the brush)

What are you doing?

NIGHTINGALE
I've got to talk to her.

JENNY
Her?

NIGHTINGALE
Proserpine. The demon who's been promised my immortal soul.

JENNY
Jack....

NIGHTINGALE
There's no other way.

JENNY
And just how are you planning to talk to this Proserpine?

JENNY remembers the books that she's holding.

JENNY
You're as mad as they are.

NIGHTINGALE
I can't do it without you.

JENNY looks resigned. She knows he's right.

INT. BASEMENT, GOSLING'S HOUSE- LATER

JENNY is looking through the notebook. NIGHTINGALE is pacing around the basement.

JENNY
For a start, the circle has to be drawn with a magic sword.

NIGHTINGALE
What?

JENNY

That's what it says. You can outline the circle with chalk, but for it to be effective, it has to be inscribed with a sword.

NIGHTINGALE
(sarcastic)
Well that's it, then. Where am I going to get a magical sword from at this time of night?

JENNY
(reading notebook)
If you can't get a magical sword, you can use a birch branch.

She smiles brightly.

EXT. GARDEN, GOSLING'S HOUSE - NIGHT

NIGHTINGALE is up a tree.

NIGHTINGALE
Are you sure this is a birch?

JENNY
Trust me, I was a Girl Guide.

NIGHTINGALE rips a branch off the tree.

INT. DINING ROOM, GOSLING'S HOUSE - LATER

JENNY is helping NIGHTINGALE draw a magic circle on the floor.

NIGHTINGALE goes over the white chalk line with the point of the birch branch.

JENNY
Then you draw a triangle outside the circle. The demon has to stay in the area between the circle and the triangle.

                    NIGHTINGALE
Okay.

                        JENNY
Wait. The apex of the triangle has to point north.

                    NIGHTINGALE
Which way is north?

JENNY thinks about it, then points.

                        JENNY
That way, I think.

                    NIGHTINGALE
You think? I thought you were a Girl Guide?

NIGHTINGALE draws the triangle as JENNY reads the
notebook.

                        JENNY
Then you have to write MI, CHA and EL at the three point
of the triangle. The letters form the name Michael.

                    NIGHTINGALE
Michael?

                        JENNY
The Archangel.

JENNY shakes her head at the madness of it.

INT. DINING ROOM, GOSLING'S HOUSE - LATER

NIGHTINGALE and JENNY place candles at the points of the
triangle. NIGHTINGALE lights them as JENNY looks through
the book.

                    NIGHTINGALE
What else?

JENNY shows him the notebook.

> JENNY
>
> You have to recite this.

She points at a crucible on the floor containing herbs.

> JENNY
>
> Then light this. And say this. Bagahi laca bacabe.

> NIGHTINGALE
>
> And that's it?

> JENNY
>
> You have to be totally spotless. Squeaky clean.

> NIGHTINGALE
>
> Because?

> JENNY
>
> Because any dirt weakens the circle. Look, I'm just telling you what it says, that's all. If the recipe's wrong, blame Delia, not me.

> NIGHTINGALE
>
> Delia?

> JENNY
>
> Delia Smith.
> (exasperated)
> Forget it.

> NIGHTINGALE
>
> Okay. I was just asking. I'm new to this too, you know.

> JENNY
>
> You're not going to go through with this, are you?

> NIGHTINGALE
>
> I don't see that I've any choice.

JENNY

Listen to yourself. You're planning on summoning the devil.

NIGHTINGALE

Not the devil. A devil.

JENNY

And assuming the whole world isn't going crazy, and you do summon this devil....what then?

NIGHTINGALE

I'll play it by ear.

JENNY shakes her head as if he's crazy.

NIGHTINGALE

You have to go now, Jenny.

JENNY

No way.

NIGHTINGALE

I have to do this on my own.

JENNY

I'm staying.

NIGHTINGALE

I don't know what's going to happen. But I do know that if it goes wrong, I don't want you around.

JENNY

You're always doing that.

NIGHTINGALE

What?

JENNY

Pushing me away.

NIGHTINGALE

It could be dangerous...

JENNY

I don't mean this.

JENNY moves towards him. She puts her hands on his shoulders.

JENNY

It's not about this. It's about you. And me. You know how I feel, Jack. I can't have made it any more obvious.

She kisses him. Hard. NIGHTINGALE responds. Then pulls away.

NIGHTINGALE

Maybe, just maybe, my soul isn't mine, Jenny. Maybe that's why I've never been able to get close to anybody my whole life. And maybe this is a way of getting my soul back. OK?

JENNY nods slowly. She understands.

NIGHTINGALE

I'll call you when it's over.

JENNY

They've got phones in Hell, have they?

JENNY shakes her head and leaves.

EXT. GOSLING'S HOUSE - NIGHT

JENNY stands looking up at the house. She wants to go back. But knows that she can't. She gets into her car.

INT. BEDROOM, GOSLING'S HOUSE - NIGHT

From the bedroom window, NIGHTINGALE watches JENNY drive away. The candles are all lit.

INT. BATHROOM, GOSLING'S HOUSE - NIGHT

The bathroom is ultra modern with a huge bath, big enough for three.

NIGHTINGALE is lying on his back, under water, holding his breath. For a long time.

He opens his eyes.

INT. BATH, NIGHTINGALE'S POV - NIGHT

NIGHTINGALE looks up through the water.

Something is moving. A figure. SOPHIE. Moving closer. Her hair hanging down over her face.

Moving closer to the bath. Closer. Closer.

INT. BATHROOM, GOSLING'S HOUSE - NIGHT

NIGHTINGALE sits up, the breath exploding from his lungs. Water splashes over the floor.

He looks around. There's no-one there. He's alone in the bathroom. He wipes his face.

INT. DINING ROOM, GOSLING'S HOUSE - NIGHT

A squeaky clean NIGHTINGALE steps inside the circle.

He looks around the room. Then he starts to read from Jenny's notebook.

The candles flicker. A wind blows through the room even though the windows are firmly shut.

NIGHTINGALE looks around. He carries on reading Latin from the notebook.

More wind. Then a reality itself seems to flicker. NIGHTINGALE bends down and ignites the contents of the crucible. A thick plume of smoke arises from it.

He looks up. The room is flickering now, moving in and out of reality.

Then there's a figure in the room with him. Jet black hair. Pale white skin. Lots of piercings. Lots of black eyeshadow and black lipstick. Demons choose the form that they appear in, and this is PROSERPINE's appearance of choice.

She speaks with a deep, throaty voice. Almost masculine.

> PROSERPINE
> Jack Nightingale.
> (beat)
> Are you in such a hurry to join me?

> NIGHTINGALE
> You're Proserpine? Princess of Hell?

> PROSERPINE
> Do you want to see my ID?

She laughs, slowly stalking around the circle. NIGHTINGALE turns with her, always facing her.

> PROSERPINE
> You expected horns? A forked tail? The stench of brimstone?

She laughs. NIGHTINGALE takes out his packet of cigarettes.

> NIGHTINGALE
> Do you want a cigarette? I guess cancer isn't an option for you.

PROSERPINE laughs, pleased that he's recognised her.

He's about to light his cigarette, but then he stops. She's watching him, carefully.

> NIGHTINGALE
> Smoke's an impurity, isn't it? It would weaken the circle.

> PROSERPINE
> Maybe. Try it and see.

NIGHTINGALE puts the cigarette away.

She examines the things around him. The book. The chalice. The herbs. She nods approvingly.

> PROSERPINE
> You've read Mitchell's book?

> NIGHTINGALE
> My father had it.

> PROSERPINE
> Didn't do him any good. The contract is inviolable. Written in his blood. And you bear the mark.

She carries on walking around the circle, but staying within the triangle. NIGHTINGALE keeps watching her. Trying to stay cool. She looks like a teenager but she's a demon from hell and not to be trusted.

> NIGHTINGALE
> Deals can be broken.

> PROSERPINE
> Not this one. Your soul is mine.

> NIGHTINGALE
> Mitchell seems to think he's won.

PROSERPINE sneers at him.

PROSERPINE
The fat lady hasn't sung yet.

NIGHTINGALE
He says so long as he dies in the circle, he enters hell under
his own terms.

PROSERPINE
We'll see.
(a beat)
Maybe I will have a cigarette.

PROSERPINE holds out her hand. NIGHTINGALE takes out the
pack and hands it to her. Just before she touches the packet he
pulls back, realising that any physical contact is dangerous.

She laughs, knowing that she almost had him.

He tosses her the pack and she catches it effortlessly. She takes
out a cigarette and throws the pack back at him.

PROSERPINE
(in a young girl's voice)
Got a light, mister?

It's the voice that called out just before HOYLE was hit by the
van.

PROSERPINE laughs and holds out her hand. It bursts into
flames and she uses it to light the cigarette. She exhales smoke,
then the flames vanish from her hand.

PROSERPINE
Are you scared, Nightingale?

NIGHTINGALE says nothing.

PROSERPINE
You should be.

She stares at him. Suddenly NIGHTINGALE realises that there is something at his feet. Snakes. Lots of snakes. Big ones, small ones, all swirling around him. They start to climb his feet.

NIGHTINGALE fights to control himself. This can't be real.

PROSERPINE smiles.

Suddenly the ground around the circle erupts and it hurtles upwards through the ceiling. Through the bedroom. Through the roof.

NIGHTINGALE and PROSERPINE face each other as the floor they are standing on soars upwards. Then they stop.

The wind blows around them. They are so, so, so, high, standing on a thin column of rock.

PROSERPINE

Scared now?

NIGHTINGALE

This isn't real.

PROSERPINE

What is, Nightingale? You think your puny life on earth is real, do you?

She laughs. Then the floor starts to fall and the column of rock withdraws, taking them with it. They go back down, in reverse, as if time is being played backwards. Down through the sky. Through the house. Then there's just silence as they face each other. NIGHTINGALE in the circle, PROSERPINE outside. The ceiling is as it should be, as if it never happened.

PROSERPINE

Hell. Now hell is real.

Reality flickers.

EXT. HELL - DAY/NIGHT/who knows?

NIGHTINGALE is in Hell. There are DEMONS, there are
SOULS being tortured, fire, lava, steam. It's Hell, or a version of
Hell that PROSERPINE wants him to see.

> PROSERPINE
> Imagine an eternity here, Nightingale.
> (a beat)
> Welcome to your future.

NIGHTINGALE stares at PROSERPINE. He can't bring himself
to look at the horror around him and he knows that if he takes his
eyes off her, he'll be lost forever.

PROSERPINE smiles and reality flickers again.

INT. DINING ROOM, GOSLING'S HOUSE - NIGHT

NIGHTINGALE is in the circle and PROSERPINE is outside it.
NIGHTINGALE is scared, but resolute.

> PROSERPINE
> Come to me now, Jack. I'll make it easier for you. More...
> Bearable.

> NIGHTINGALE
> I'm staying here. You can't touch me here and you know it.

> PROSERPINE
> Maybe.

> JENNY (O.S.)
> Jack?

NIGHTINGALE looks to the side. JENNY is standing there,
looking confused.

> JENNY

Jack, what's happening?

> NIGHTINGALE
> Jenny?

Suddenly JENNY flies back through the air, arms outstretched, and splatters against the wall.

> JENNY

Jack!

Blood trickles from her nose. Some invisible force is pressing against her, crushing her, spread-eagled against the wall. One by one, her bones start to crack.

NIGHTINGALE moves towards her, then stops as he realises that he's about to leave the circle. He stares at JENNY, watches as the life is crushed from her.

Then he turns to look at PROSERPINE. He stares at her with cold eyes.

> NIGHTINGALE

This isn't real.

> PROSERPINE

Are you sure?

> NIGHTINGALE

I'm sure.

> PROSERPINE
> Would you bet your life on that? Would you bet her life?

NIGHTINGALE thinks about it. Then nods.

PROSERPINE smiles. And JENNY vanishes.

PROSERPINE paces around the circle, thinking.

PROSERPINE

So what's this all about? You want to beg for your immortal soul, is that it?

NIGHTINGALE

No.

PROSERPINE stops pacing. That's not the answer she expected.

NIGHTINGALE

I'm not here to beg.
                    (a beat)
I'm here to negotiate.

PROSERPINE starts to laugh. The whole room begins to shake as if in the grip of an earthquake.

EXT. MITCHELL'S HOUSE - DAY

NIGHTINGALE drives up to MITCHELL's house.

He presses the intercom.

NIGHTINGALE

Tell Mitchell it's Jack Nightingale. Tell him I've got an answer to his problem.

On the passenger seat is an old book and an old leather bag.

INT. MAIN ROOM, MITCHELL'S HOUSE - DAY

The SEVERE WOMAN escorts NIGHTINGALE to where MITCHELL is sitting in his protective circle. NIGHTINGALE is carrying the old book.

SEVERE WOMAN

I don't have to remind you of the house rules.

The TWO ARMED MEN keep a close eye on NIGHTINGALE.
One of them is carrying the old leather bag that was in the car.

MITCHELL takes the oxygen mask away from his face.

> MITCHELL
> Haven't you got anything better to do? The clock's ticking,
> isn't it?

> NIGHTINGALE
> I'm here to help you.

> MITCHELL
> I don't need your help. Tonight's the night, isn't it? One
> minute past midnight and it's all over.

> NIGHTINGALE
> I know what to do now. I know how to stop Proserpine.

> MITCHELL
> She can't be stopped. She has too much power.

NIGHTINGALE holds up the book.

> NIGHTINGALE
> It's in here.

MITCHELL shakes his head.

> NIGHTINGALE
> You can help me. With the power you have, we can bring
> her down.

> NIGHTINGALE
> She sits on the right hand of Satan. She's beyond all attacks.

NIGHTINGALE shakes his head.

> NIGHTINGALE
> We can do it.

> MITCHELL

I'm not leaving the circle.

> NIGHTINGALE

Then I'll do it on my own.

NIGHTINGALE nods at the window, overlooking the garden.

> NIGHTINGALE

Out there.

> MITCHELL

How?

> NIGHTINGALE

A dagger. A dagger that has been given but not thanked for.

NIGHTINGALE holds out his hand for the bag. The ARMED MAN gives it to NIGHTINGALE.

NIGHTINGALE opens the bag and takes out the knife.

The TWO ARMED MEN point their weapons at NIGHTINGALE.

NIGHTINGALE holds up his hands, showing that he isn't a threat.

> MITCHELL
> (to the ARMED MEN)

It's okay.
> (to NIGHTINGALE)

That's your father's?

> NIGHTINGALE

He had it. And he had the book that explains how it's to be used. But it can only be used when she appears in human form. When she comes to claim a soul.

MITCHELL shakes his head.

MITCHELL
She's too strong.

NIGHTINGALE
What have I got to lose? Help me.

MITCHELL
I'm not leaving this circle. Not until I die.

NIGHTINGALE
Suit yourself.

EXT. GARDEN, MITCHELL'S HOUSE - DAY

NIGHTINGALE walks across the lawn towards a paved patio area.

MITCHELL is watching from the house, through the huge window.

NIGHTINGALE puts the bag down and opens it.

INT. MAIN ROOM, MITCHELL'S HOUSE - DAY

MITCHELL watches as NIGHTINGALE takes out white chalk and starts to draw a pentangle.

SEVERE WOMAN
We could throw him out, Sir.

MITCHELL holds up his hand. He wants to see what happens.

He watches as NIGHTINGALE works on his pentangle.

MITCHELL
He's drawing a pentangle. He's crazy. It has to be a circle. A circle with a triangle. She'll rip him apart.

INT. GARDEN, MITCHELL'S HOUSE - DAY

NIGHTINGALE is putting the finishes to the pentangle.

INT. MAIN ROOM, MITCHELL'S HOUSE - DAY

As MITCHELL and the SEVERE WOMAN watch, NIGHTINGALE sits down in the middle of the pentangle with the book in his hands.

> SEVERE WOMAN
> What's he doing now?

> MITCHELL
> Waiting. For midnight.

EXT. GARDEN, MITCHELL'S HOUSE - NIGHT

NIGHTINGALE looks at his wristwatch. Midnight. He stands up.

He looks around the garden. The wind starts to pick up. A dog howls. He shivers.

INT. MAIN ROOM, MITCHELL'S HOUSE - NIGHT

MITCHELL is looking at a digital clock on the wall. It clicks over to midnight..

MITCHELL, the SEVERE WOMAN and the TWO ARMED MEN, watch through the window.

EXT. GARDEN, MITCHELL'S HOUSE - NIGHT

Reality flickers. Then PROSERPINE is there. Grinning.

                    PROSERPINE
        Time to pay the piper, Nightingale.

NIGHTINGALE starts to read from the old book. It's Latin.

PROSERPINE grins. She paces up and down.

                    PROSERPINE
        You're wasting your breath.

NIGHTINGALE continues to read from the book.

PROSERPINE folds her arms and stares at NIGHTINGALE with
contempt.

INT. MAIN ROOM, MITCHELL'S HOUSE - NIGHT

MITCHELL, the SEVERE WOMAN and the TWO ARMED
MEN watch as PROSERPINE sneers at NIGHTINGALE.

                    MITCHELL
        He's got balls, all right.
                    (a beat)
        But he's as good as dead.

NIGHTINGALE hands the book to PROSERPINE.

                    MITCHELL
        No! Never allow contact!

As they watch, PROSERPINE takes the book.

Suddenly NIGHTINGALE produces a knife and plunges it into
PROSERPINE's heart.

                    MITCHELL
        My God!

The oxygen mask falls from MITCHELL's hand and he gets to
his feet.

PROSERPINE is in agony. Lightning flashes.

NIGHTINGALE steps back into the centre of the pentangle.

PROSERPINE slumps to the floor.

> MITCHELL
>
> He's done it.

EXT. GARDEN, MITCHELL'S HOUSE - NIGHT

NIGHTINGALE stands looking over the body of PROSERPINE.

The wind is roaring. Lightning flashes.

NIGHTINGALE steps out of the circle.

INT. MAIN ROOM, MITCHELL'S HOUSE - NIGHT

MITCHELL watches as NIGHTINGALE stands over the body of PROSERPINE.

MITCHELL steps unsteadily out of his circle, towards the window.

> MITCHELL
>
> How did he do that? Sixty years I've studied...sixty years and I couldn't have accomplished that.

EXT. GARDEN, MITCHELL'S HOUSE - NIGHT

The storm is building, whipping at NIGHTINGALE's hair.

He hears a voice.

> MITCHELL
>
> Nightingale!

NIGHTINGALE turns to see MITCHELL walking unsteadily across the lawn.

The SEVERE WOMAN and the TWO ARMED MEN watch from the window.

> MITCHELL
> My God! I don't believe it!

NIGHTINGALE lights a cigarette and watches as MITCHELL walks across the lawn. MITCHELL is animated. Excited.

> MITCHELL
> You did it, man! You did it.

> NIGHTINGALE
> Yeah. I did it.

NIGHTINGALE blows smoke.

MITCHELL reaches him and hugs him.

> MITCHELL
> You killed her! How did you do it? How in God's name did you do it?

> PROSERPINE
> God had nothing to do with it.

MITCHELL freezes. PROSERPINE floats to her feet. She's not dead. Most definitely not dead. She pulls out the knife and tosses it away. She laughs. The laugh of a triumphant demon. The ground shakes.

MITCHELL stares at her. Then he stares at NIGHTINGALE as he realises what has just happened.

He moves towards the pentangle then realises that it won't do any good. He stops.

MITCHELL
You set me up.

NIGHTINGALE
I did a deal. That's what I do. I negotiate.

PROSERPINE
I've waited for you for a long time, Mitchell.

MITCHELL
(to NIGHTINGALE)
You bastard!

NIGHTINGALE
Sticks and stones.

MITCHELL starts to run. PROSERPINE laughs. A hole appears in the ground. Flames. Fire. Brimstone. Demons. They drag a screaming MITCHELL down into the fires of hell.

As the hole seals up, the storm quietens.

PROSERPINE
I do hate long good-byes.

PROSERPINE smiles at NIGHTINGALE.

PROSERPINE
Many happy returns, Jack Nightingale.

She blows him a kiss. She turns and starts to walk away.

NIGHTINGALE
Wait!

PROSERPINE stops but doesn't turn around. When she speaks, it's not a girl's voice. It's the voice of a devil.

PROSERPINE

Do not try my patience, Nightingale. You are not inside a protective circle now.

NIGHTINGALE

The girl.

PROSERPINE turns slowly.

PROSERPINE

Tread carefully. You're not the boss of me.

NIGHTINGALE

I know who your boss is.
(a beat)
The girl. Sophie. What happens to her?

PROSERPINE laughs. The laugh is deep and echoes. It's not a human laugh.

PROSERPINE

Your concern is so... touching.

NIGHTINGALE

What happens to her?

PROSERPINE

Why do you care?

NIGHTINGALE

I care. She's just a kid.

PROSERPINE

Was a kid. Now she's just a soul.
(a beat)
But not one of ours, Nightingale.

PROSERPINE looks off to the side. SOPHIE is standing there. She looks prettier now. The dark patches under her eyes have gone. She isn't so pale. Her hair is glossier.

NIGHTINGALE looks over at SOPHIE.

NIGHTINGALE raises his hand and gives SOPHIE a small wave. There are no words. She smiles, a little. It's a worried smile, but it's a smile.

She slowly waves back. Then the night sky above her glows, and she vanishes.

NIGHTINGALE lights a cigarette and looks at PROSERPINE.

                    NIGHTINGALE
This was all planned, wasn't it? From the start?

                    PROSERPINE
It worked out all right in the end, didn't it?

                    NIGHTINGALE
You got what you wanted.

                    PROSERPINE
And you got your soul back. All's well that ends well.

                    NIGHTINGALE
You used me. To get Mitchell.

                    PROSERPINE
It was your idea. Remember?

                    NIGHTINGALE
Was it? Was it really?

PROSERPINE blows him a kiss and walks away. Reality flickers and she's gone.

NIGHTINGALE takes a long pull on his cigarette and blows smoke.

                    NIGHTINGALE
  That went well.

NIGHTINGALE turns and walks away from the house.

Fade out:

20966834R00091

Printed in Great Britain
by Amazon